Reprisal

Alfie Robins

Kings Town Publishing

First Published by Taylor Street Publishing. 2011.

3rd Edition, Kings Town Publishing, 2016.

British Library Cataloguing in Publication Data
A CIP catalogue record for this book is available from the British Library

ISBN: 978-0-9927594-3-8

About the Author

Alfie Robins was born and raised in the English east coast city of Kingston Upon Hull, known locally as, 'Ull. Alfie left school at 15 and started work as a ships carpenter working on the trawlers on Hull fish dock. Over the years he has had a varied career, carpenter, production manager in the caravan industry and sales manager with a radio communications company, to name but a few. He is now retired and concentrates on his writing.

Alfie has three grown up children, two grandchildren and lives with his wife and son in rural East Yorkshire, England.

Also by Alfie Robins

Snakes and Losers

Why Won't You Stay Dead

Just Whistle

Funeral Rites

To be published in 2016

Suits and Bullets

A Winning Hand Loses

Acknowledgements

I would like to give special thanks to my family for their encouragement and support during the process of writing this book.

My daughters for keeping me pointed in the right direction, my son for cheering me up when the writing was tough, and my wife for putting up with me constantly going on about characters and plots.

The novel is based on the present day Hull, and Hull as it used to be during its heyday as the UK's premier fishing port. I might add, with also a little help from my imagination.

For Lee

Reprisal

Chapter 1

The wind blew in off the River Humber, whipping up the surface of the enclosed Princes Dock in the centre of town. The black water erupted into a series of waves that smashed against the dockside. An unwelcome spray of stagnant water soaked the winter clothing of the office workers and early morning shoppers as they went about their business.

This January morning was typical for the North East of England - dark, cold, damp and miserable.

In the warmth of Hull's Police Headquarters, DCI Philip Marlowe, along with a number of his counterparts from around the area, occupied the conference room with cold cups of tea and coffee in front of them, leaving rings on the highly polished mahogany table. Each and every officer looked as pissed off as Marlowe himself felt.

Chief Superintendent Bulmer, all starched and stiff in his best dress uniform with its shiny silver buttons, had stood at the head of the table droning on over statistics for the past forty minutes.

'Well, gentlemen, I hope you have all taken on board what has been said this morning...,' Bulmer said in his precise and proper voice as he scanned the faces looking for the slightest sign of interest. '... and that, gentlemen, concludes today's meeting.'

The Chief Superintendent picked up his files and tapped them on all four edges to keep them square and level. With his cap tucked underneath his arm, he once more looked around the room at the early morning faces, nodded and left the room.

'Thank heavens for that,' a voice from the other end of the table announced.

'I'll second that,' quipped Inspector Bob Allan, who sat next to Marlowe.

'Fancy another coffee, Phil?' Allan asked.

'No thanks, Bob. I'm dying for a fag and I'd better get back to see what the troops are up to.'

* * *

DCI Philip Marlowe wasn't too happy as he left the warmth of the building and stepped into the cold and rain. For as long as he could remember he had always wanted to be a copper, but days like these made him wish he had chosen a different career. He had been summoned to attend a breakfast meeting concerning budgets, targets and the last quarter's 'clear up' rates, the part of the job he hated.

Breakfast meeting? It was more like the middle of the bloody night, the DCI thought. It was 8.30 a.m. and he had been there since 6.00 a.m.

Marlowe walked out through the main entrance doors and placed his briefcase on the floor as he fumbled in his pocket for his cigarettes. 'Another bloody smoke. How many is this today?' He mumbled to himself as he hunched his shoulders and pulled up the collar of his wax jacket, tucking his neck in. Turning away from the wind blowing straight across Queens Gardens, he cupped his hands, flicked his lighter, lit the cigarette and sucked hungrily, enjoying the quick hit of nicotine. He reached down, picked up his briefcase and started to walk away from Hull's Central Police station.

With his back to the wind, he made his way to his car, a five year old black Ford Mondeo, his own car. The DCI wasn't keen on police pool cars, his theory being you never knew what infectious diseases you might catch from them. Marlowe had left the Mondeo in the adjacent multi storey car park, a typical concrete structure built in the sixties. Not trusting the claustrophobic, evil-smelling lift, he made his way up the narrow concrete stairwell to level 3. There was no way he could avoid the stink of stale beer, cigarettes and urine that clung to the concrete, so he quickened his step in haste to reach the moderately fresh petrol-fumed air of level 3. He took the keys out of his pocket, pressed the remote fob, listened for the click and headed in the direction of the noise.

Marlowe opened the door and lowered himself into the driving seat. Just as he was about to turn on the ignition, his mobile phone burst into life. He put the phone in the hands-free and pressed the accept key. 'DCI Marlowe.'

'Boss, its Gowan. Are you on the way back?' DI Gowan was Marlowe's second in command.

'Just about to leave now. What's the problem?'

'The body of a young bloke has turned up. Uniform are on the scene,' replied Detective Inspector Dave Gowan.

'Ok, Dave. I'll see you shortly.'

He ended the call and carefully manoeuvred out of the parking space, heading towards the exit. Following the direction of the arrows, Marlowe negotiated his way through the tight sequence of right hand turns that led to life outside of the concrete box.

* * *

The Gordon Street Community Station was an old station dating back to the late nineteenth century, a three storey grey brick Victorian building with a grey slate roof and blue paintwork. The station still retained many original architectural features on the exterior; it even had the blue lamp hanging above the main entrance, not that it always worked. For many years the station had been run on a shoestring budget, but now, in the days of visible community policing, it had been given a new lease of life.

In comparison to the building's exterior, the inside of the nick was a different picture. It could be described as 'state of the art' as far as local stations went. The ultra-modern reception area was manned by a Civilian Support Officer and the station even had refurbished cells for its 'clients'.

Marlowe turned left and eased the Mondeo into the small car park twenty minutes after leaving Central. He was relieved to find that nobody had stolen his parking place. Even though his name was clearly marked on the wall, it was most unusual to find the space vacant.

Marlowe took the keys from the ignition and climbed out, locked the car, and walked across to the rear door of the station, keying in the security code, grateful to step into the warmth of Custody reception.

'Morning, Trev,' Marlowe called to the Custody sergeant. Sergeant Trevor Cleeves was an experienced officer with twenty years' service behind him, a good copper and an old friend of the DCIs. Cleeves couldn't wait for retirement.

The sergeant looked up from his paperwork. 'Morning, Magnum. They managed to get hold of you, then? Running round like headless chickens back there. No control, your lot!'

'Don't take the piss, Trev, it's too early.'

Trev smirked to himself, put his head down and carried on checking the custody sheet from the previous evening as Marlowe passed through the Custody area.

'Boss,' DI Dave Gowan said, nodding to the DCI as he walked into the squad room.

'Morning all,' Marlowe shouted out as they both walked towards his office. There wasn't much of an enthusiastic welcome, just a few nods and moans. The squad room was like the rest of the station - classy, of an open design, airy and with plenty of room between the desks. As far as DCIs' offices went, Marlowe couldn't grumble. His personal space was a quite large partitioned-off glass section of the main squad room with vertical blinds for when privacy was required.

When Marlowe had first seen the new layout, he had thought it was lacking any character. He'd soon stamped his own bit of individuality on the place. He bought a new cd player for on the filing cabinet, a glass-topped coffee table and a small two-seater sofa. He'd even brought in a cheap coffee making machine.

Marlowe took off his waxed jacket, hung it on the chrome coat stand and turned to face his colleague.

5

'What have we got, then, Dave?' He moved around his desk, gesturing for Gowan to sit. As he did so, Gowan dropped the buff coloured folder he was carrying onto the coffee table. The DCI lowered himself into his comfy worn leather chair and settled back. One thing he'd insisted on during the revamp was keeping his old soggy chair.

Gowan shifted his tall frame in the deep cushions of the sofa and smoothed down the creases in his already wrinkled suit trousers. Marlowe smiled to himself; the DI looked almost comical on the low sofa with his knees sticking up in the air.

'A call came through saying that they had found the body of a man on the old riverside quay, you know, the one that runs along the perimeter of the new Humber Business Park.'

'I know where you mean, at the back of Albert Dock. Natural causes?'

'Bloody strange if it was, unless he wrapped himself in plastic sheeting first,' Gowan replied as he stretched out his long legs.

'Who called it in?' Marlowe took out his spectacles and dropped them on the desk.

'Local security firm, Pride Securities.'

'I've heard of them. What's the state of play so far? Who's down there?'

'Uniform got to the scene as soon as it was reported. Once it was confirmed, I sent Jenny to see what's going on and coordinate until we get down there.'

Marlowe ignored the flashing emails on his computer screen as he listened. 'Ok, check with Jenny that there's enough uniforms to contain the scene, then get yourself down there. Take the young trainee from uniform with you. I've a couple of things to sort, then I'll be with you.'

'Ok, Boss, I'm on the way. Lee! Here, now!' Marlowe's eardrums came close to bursting as Gowan yelled to the trainee DC even before he shut the door to the office behind him. Marlowe cringed. TDC Lee Kristianson, short and stocky with sticking up blonde hair with a mind of its own, was the latest recruit to the squad, a trainee still in his first month with the team.

DCI Marlowe picked up the file DI Gowan had left relating to the other incidents that had occurred the previous night and flicked through it. Nothing too taxing, he thought, as the computer screen still flickered at him - a break-in at a 'Booze Buster', a couple of household burglaries and the usual drunken assaults. Nothing that Uniform couldn't sort out until he got back from the quay.

Feeling worn out already from his early start, he pushed back the chair and ran his hand across his stubble chin. 'Another day, another dollar,' he mumbled aloud. He stood up, removed his coat from the chrome stand and put it on. Then he checked his pockets - car keys, mobile phone, all there. He also picked up his Motorola Airwaves radio out of the charger and stuffed it in his jacket pocket. He'd only been in the office twenty minutes. What a bloody good start to the week, he thought. He went back through the Custody area, heading for the car park.

This time Sergeant Cleeves kept quiet and his head down.

* * *

7

The DCI unlocked the car and climbed in. Fastening his seatbelt, he turned the ignition on and eased the Mondeo out of the car park, heading for the riverfront. He drove south up the tree-lined Boulevard and turned right onto Hessle Road. Even this early in the morning the shoppers were already out along what was once the busiest shopping area in Hull during the fishing years.

Marlowe was stopped again at the traffic lights at the corner of Westdock Avenue to let a gaggle of shoppers hurry across with their heads bent down and their arms stretched with heavy shopping. He turned the Mondeo left, down by the side of the Star and Garter public house. For as long as Marlowe could remember, the Star and Garter had been locally known as 'Rayners', after an old landlord. Its claim to fame was that it was supposed to have the longest bar in the city. At the junction with Gaulton Street he crossed and entered the old fish dock underpass with water dripping through its tiled sides and its roof seeping from the land above. Marlowe had fond memories of walking through the tunnel as a child. His father had worked on the trawlers, and he and his mother had had to make a weekly pilgrimage to the ship owner's office to collect his father's wages. Marlowe could remember shouting as loud as he could in the tunnel. The echoes were fantastic.

Not so many years ago, the old riverside quay had been a busy, thriving part of the local economy, lined with Wilson Line coasters that plied their trade between the East Coast and Baltic ports. Timber for the caravan industry had been the main import for this particular wharf which now lay semi-derelict, with just the odd coaster making an appearance. The majority of the sheds on the quay were being occupied by small start-up, low rent, businesses, easy in and easy out.

The quay area was a hive of activity when Marlowe pulled up at the cordoned-off area. He parked the Mondeo away from the immediate vicinity and turned off the lights and wipers, then reached into the glove compartment and pulled out a woolly hat and a scarf. With the black and amber Hull City scarf wrapped around his neck and the woolly hat pulled down over his head and ears, Marlowe braved the elements. The sea gulls screeched and swooped overhead, gliding on the under-currents of the wind. It felt like it was blowing a gale as the penetrating wind blew the rain almost horizontally off the Humber, it was so dark and miserable. 'It should be light now. Roll on summer,' he muttered to himself. It was hard to believe it was 9 a.m. As Marlowe well knew, the unfavourable weather wasn't uncommon for this time of year on the East coast.

Standing to one side for a few moments, the DCI surveyed the scene. Rows of empty warehouses ran down one side. It was evident a number of them were boarded up with 'For Let' signs fixed to the doors. It looked like they'd not been in use for a long time. A wet, shiny cobbled road, with disused rusting railway lines, ran down the centre, separating the quayside from the buildings. Blue and white plastic incident tape had been tied around the bollards set into the cobbles, cordoning off the crime scene around 'Crane 52' which rose eerily from the quay.

DS Jenny Bright was the first to see the DCI arrive. In contrast to her usual smart-casual appearance, Bright looked like a drowned rat, as she walked across with the hood of her bright blue anorak over her head.

'Morning, Jenny. Let's go and have a look at what we've got.'

'Right you are, Boss.' She wiped the rain from her face and led the way to Crane 52. It was a struggle under foot as they clambered through the debris of scrap metal, railway sleepers and rusting chains that cluttered the quay. Marlowe thought whoever dumped the body would have had an even bigger struggle than they were having. The early morning daylight ascended slowly, holding back the weak winter sun, giving the riverside cranes the guise of grotesque prehistoric predators in the glow of the still lit overhead neon lights.

The DCI tilted his head skywards. The cranes stretched out their limbs, casting long shadows that reflected further on the wet cobbled surface of the quayside. Away from the central working area of the Quay, Crane 52 stood still and erect, a cold steel mechanical structure devoid of any feelings, towering above the murky waters of the River Humber, oblivious to the activity around its metal legs. Stretched out on the cobbles below the crane was another inanimate object wrapped in a plastic sheet, only this was of the human form, unmoving, still and lifeless.

The first officers on the scene had had enough sense to erect a temporary tarpaulin tent over the body in an effort to try and preserve any evidence from the driving rain. It was time to have a look, not Marlowe's favourite part of the job. Over the years he had seen the lot, but it never got any easier. Carefully checking each footstep, he approached the body, getting as close to the victim as was practically possible, but not too close. He didn't want a bollocking from the Scene of Crime Officer when he arrived. The DCI found that first impressions were imperative, no matter how disturbing they might be. Marlowe's philosophy was get to the scene quickly before all and sundry turned up, and you could get a better sense of what was going on, not that you could make much sense of a murder scene.

The lifeless body of a young white male, half-wrapped in plastic sheeting, lay beneath the metal limbs of the crane. Marlowe observed that the plastic around the victim's head hadn't held tight and he could see the pale face of the murdered man. He didn't look very old, probably in his late twenties or early thirties. Through the flapping plastic, Marlowe could see the body was dressed in cheap, but reasonably decent, clothes. The zip front leather bomber jacket was slightly open, a sticky substance clinging around the main body of the jacket, beneath which he wore a navy blue sweatshirt with a 'crown' motif on the front and modern faded-style denim jeans with designer rips.

The DCI dug into his jacket and pulled a pair of gloves from his pocket, stretching the latex over his fingers as he stared down at the victim. Beneath the plastic there looked to be a trace of adhesive around both ankles. The one thing he couldn't miss was the smell of urine; the poor sod had obviously pissed himself at some point. The top of his head was a congealed mass of blood. Marlowe couldn't see much evidence of trauma through the dark hair. His blood, diluted by the rain, ran in streaks across his face. Adhesive tape covered his mouth and blood was starting to leak through at the edges.

11

Marlowe thought it too risky to take a closer look without disturbing any evidence that might be there. Out the corner of his eye, he saw the SOCO team approaching, dressed in their white coveralls. He stood up and glanced down for one final look at the body. The coppery odour of blood mixing with the urine reached his nostrils and the sheer look of terror in the still-opened eyes held his gaze.

Marlowe stood up, flexed his knees and made his way to the edge of the crime scene to give the SOCOs room to work.

'Who found the body?' he asked DS Bright.

'Uniform said it was the site Security Officer. He's in the site office. I left Lee keeping an eye on him,' Jenny replied without hesitation.

The rain was still blowing in from across the river and Marlowe wiped the rain from his face. He could see more uniformed officers had arrived on the scene to make a painstaking search for any evidence the weather had not obliterated. At least the lucky buggers had their wet gear on.

'Come on, then, let's see if we can scrounge a cup of tea and see what the security guy has to say.' Marlowe turned to DI Gowan. 'Dave, will you have a word with the Forensic people? We'll be at the site office.'

'Right you are, Boss.' Gowan pulled the collar of his coat tighter, trying to stop the rain dripping down the back of his neck as he went in search of the SOCO.

With Jenny Bright trudging by his side, Marlowe headed towards the security office, carefully avoiding the wet pools of oily water that made the cobbled road as slippery as ice. The security office was a wood-panelled textured portable building standing on metal jacklegs. The company name, 'Pride Security', was fixed high on one side. Marlowe noticed it was only 350 metres away from the crime scene, but unfortunately with no direct view of Crane 52.

They climbed the three wooden steps, knocked on the door and walked in. The heat was overpowering. Condensation ran in rivulets down the windows. As far as portable buildings went, the actual interior of the cabin wasn't too bad, although Jenny did turn her nose up at the manky damp smell. A long melamine desk ran the full length along one side of the office. The security guard sat in front of the desk on a worn-looking wheeled typist's chair. Three plastic tubular chairs were lined up on the opposite wall next to the electric convector heater. Above the chairs was a cork notice board covered in coloured stick-it posters.

TDC Lee Kristianson jumped to his feet as they entered.

'You ok, Lee?' Marlowe enquired.

'Err, yes, thanks, sir,' was the short reply.

Marlowe unfastened his dripping coat, took the scarf from around his neck and pulled off the wet woollen hat, shaking them before placing them on a chair near the electric heater. The DCI pulled over one of the plastic chairs and sat down. 'Ok, then, Jenny, make the introductions. Who have we got here?'

'This is Alan Wright, the night security officer, the one who found the body,' she replied.

'Ok, Mr Wright, first things first. Lee, put the kettle on and make us a brew, will you, while I have a word with Mr Wright.'

13

The young DC jumped to his feet. Marlowe was sure he heard him mutter some comment under his breath as he moved towards the kitchen. Jenny unfastened her dripping coat, settled herself on one of the uncomfortable plastic chairs and took out her ring-bound notebook.

Marlowe pulled his chair closer to Wright. The DCI studied the security officer. He looked to be in his mid-forties. From his smart appearance, he guessed he was ex-Forces. He had an ordinary sort of face, strikingly round grey eyes and a sharp nose, the head topped with black wavy hair. Marlowe estimated him to be about 5 feet 10 or 11 inches tall and, judging from his muscular build, he was sure he could handle himself should the situation arise.

'Mr Wright, Alan. Is it alright to call you Alan?' Marlowe always used Christian names; he thought that it helped put witnesses at their ease. Without waiting for a reply, the DCI carried on. 'What time did you find the body?'

'About ten minutes past six this morning.' Jenny started taking notes.

'Then what did you do?' said Marlowe, taking out a handkerchief and wiping his face.

'I came straight back here and rang your lot, then rang the Pride office to tell them.'

'What time did you start your shift?'

'Ten o'clock last night. We do a twelve hour shift, ten till ten.' The guard shifted in his seat.

'Talk me through your procedure, the general routine.'

Lee brought over the drinks and put them down on the desk; Marlowe picked up the steaming mug and nodded his thanks to the TDC. Holding it in both hands, he put it to

14

his lips and sipped the scalding brew. 'Just relax. Get yourself settled, Alan. Just concentrate on what did or did not happen before you found the body.'

'The same as any other night, really, I come on at 10 p.m., signed the logbook for the shift change and checked my colleague's report. There was nothing unusual noted down.'

'What next?'

'When Frank left - Frank Turner, the guard on before me - I locked the office and started my first round of the quay.'

'Do you make your round on foot?'

'No, we do it in the van. The quay's too big to walk around.' Wright looked stressed as he continued. 'Usually it takes about thirty minutes for each section, maybe forty five minutes on a night like last night. You know, the weather.'

'Do you have stop-off points, strategic places to log?' Marlowe asked.

'Yes, as I said, it's a big site. It's divided into three sections and we always have to do a walk around specific areas.'

'How do you record your visits as you make the sweep? Written reports?'

'Nothing written down until we get back to the office. There are twelve key points in each section. It's a swipe card system - you simply swipe the card. The times and locations are automatically sent back directly to the Pride office, easy, no messing about. On top of that, the vehicles have trackers in 'em.'

'What time did you make your last sweep of the area?' Jenny interjected as she looked up from taking notes.

'As I said before, it's a big site. We don't cover the full site in one sweep. I started the sweep of this particular area at about five thirty this morning. There's no specific check point near the cranes, but we always drive around that way. It's part of the route. Anyway, I think it was around 6.10 a.m. when I saw something near 'fifty two' that looked a bit iffy, so I pulled up and got out of the van to take a look. As I got closer it was obvious it was a body, so I got back in the van bloody sharpish and called your lot on my mobile, and then rang the office.'

'Alan, think carefully, did you notice anything else that was out of the ordinary during the shift, any strange vehicles or people who should not be here during the night?'

'No, nothing. It was just an ordinary night.'

'Don't think I would call it an ordinary night, Alan, finding a dead body, do you?'

Marlowe turned to the TDC. 'Lee, you take a statement from Alan here, then go and see if you can help the DI.' Marlowe faced the security officer. 'That will do for now, Alan, but I'm sure we'll have a few questions for you later. Jenny, you come back to the station with me. Let's get the investigation moving.' Jenny slipped her notepad back into her bag. Marlowe stood and reached for his hat and scarf, and turned to the guard. 'Thanks again for your cooperation, Mr Wright,' reverting to his surname once more. 'I am sure we will meet again soon.' The DCI fastened up his jacket and reluctantly put on the still-damp hat and scarf. DS Bright picked up her shoulder bag and zipped up her waterproof coat, pulling the non-flattering hood over her head as she followed the DCI out into the elements once more.

The rain was still coming down steadily when TDC Kristianson reached Crane 52. DI Dave Gowan was standing patiently watching the SOCO examiners' search of the immediate vicinity from the outside of the blue and white plastic taped perimeter. The rain was running down the back of the neck of his high visibility waterproof coat.

'The Boss sent me. Anything I can do?'

'No, not yet. Brice said he'll speak with us in a few minutes.' Brice was the senior SOCO on duty, a very thorough officer who worked closely with the investigation teams. According to Brice, the job of the SOCO was to find the clues to the "how" not the "why", which was their responsibility. Nevertheless, it never stopped him from making suggestions that could be somewhat irritating at times. Within two minutes of Kristianson arriving at Crane 52, Bill Brice was over. He and his team were covered from head to foot in dripping wet white plastic suits and overshoes to prevent any contamination of evidence, unlike the crime scene investigators portrayed in the popular CSI television programmes. Looking like he'd just stepped out of a sci-fi film, he walked across to greet the two detectives.

'Dave, how are you doing? I haven't seen you for a while. How's the love life?' Brice said as he bent down to pass under the plastic tape, leaving his team to carry on processing the site.

'Not too bad, Bill. As for the love life - what's that? What can you tell us?'

17

'He's dead,' Brice dead-panned. 'First impression is he looks in quite good nick for a dead bloke. I will be able to tell you more when we get him back and take the wrapper off. Did you see the congealed blood on the top of the head?' Gowan nodded. 'Very interesting, I poked about a bit in his hair, and guess what. There's a flat piece of metal about a centimetre in diameter embedded in the hair, tight to the scalp.' Brice left the sentence hanging.

'Go on, then, what is it?' sighed the DI.

'Well, believe it or not, it looks like the head of a wire nail compressed to his skull. Never seen anything like it before.' Smiling now in a macabre sort of way, he carried on. 'I would stake my reputation on it that it was the nail that killed him, a bloody nail hammered right into his brain. Quite interesting.'

'What about a time of death?' Gowan asked.

'I can only give an estimate. Rigor hasn't set in yet. Body temperature drops at one and a half degrees an hour and, allowing for the air temperature combined with the weather being like it is, I can only guess at this stage - probably around three this morning. The pathologist will be able to give a more accurate time after the post-mortem.' Brice had a broad grin on his face. 'Can't wait for the x-ray, I'd like to know how long that bloody nail is! Oh, by the way, this is what we found in his pockets. Not much, I'm afraid.' He passed over a clear plastic evidence bag containing a wallet, car keys, mobile phone and some loose change, then, almost abruptly, turned around, said 'Cheerio,' and ducked back under the plastic tape to carry on with the processing of the scene.

18

'Saw that on telly once.' Lee piped up.

The DI looked puzzled. 'Saw what?'

'A bloke with a nail in his head. It was in one of the *Sharpe* series on television, somewhere out in India. This big bloke, an executioner, hammered a nail into the top a man's head with his fist.'

The DI was gobsmacked and shook his head in disbelief. 'Thanks for that, Lee. That should narrow it down quite a bit. So we are looking for a sixteenth century Indian torturer, are we? That shouldn't be too difficult. Can't be many of them in Hull!'

The sky was starting to get lighter but, the rain showed no sign of easing; it was still heaving it down. By this time there were a few more people coming onto the quay, heading for work and taking more than a passing interest in events. A small crowd had started to gather in the distance, taking in what they would later watch Gordon Clarke reporting on 'Look North', the local news television station. The two Detectives, already wet through, tried to wrap themselves into their coats for protection against the elements but with no luck. The wind was sending a sticky, salty spray to mingle in with the rain. Trudging through the puddles, they headed to the unmarked police car, an unobtrusive blue Peugeot 307 parked some 50 metres away. Gowan passed the young TDC the car keys and walked around to the passenger side.

'You drive, I pick the music,' Gowan said to the young detective. 'Let's get back and see what the Boss has to say. Don't know about you, but I'm ready for a bacon sarnie. My stomach thinks my throat's been cut.'

With the blower on full trying to clear the condensation, and the windscreen wipers slapping away the Humber drizzle in time with the music, the two detectives made their way back to the station.

Chapter 2

DCI Marlowe stood at the front of the functional squad office with his back to the white board on which had been placed an aerial view of the quay area alongside the first digital photographs taken at the scene.

'OK,' he said, looking around the assembled team. 'I've been designated the Senior Investigating Officer for this one.' Marlowe turned towards his DI. 'Dave, talk us through what we have got so far.'

Dave Gowan, refreshed from a quick coffee and a bite to eat, stood up from his chair and eased his way between the desks. On reaching the front, he turned to face the team. 'As you all should know by now, a suspicious death was called in at around six fifteen this morning.' He watched the faces of the team as he pointed to the photograph of the plastic wrapped corpse that had been fastened to the board. 'Initial examination at the scene shows an injury to the head being the probable cause of death. We won't know any more until the pathologist has a look at him. Going back to the head injury, according to Brice he may have been killed by a wire nail hammered into the skull and penetrating the brain. As I said, we will have to wait for more information.

The toxicology report and the post mortem will give more precise information.' This produced a few murmurs through the room. 'Anyway, to carry on, the body was found by the security guard on the site, Alan Wright. As of yet we have very little other information to go on.'

'Any other witnesses?' said a voice belonging to DC Tanya Etherington. Tanya was about 5 foot 5 inches tall with an intelligent face and shoulder length fair hair. Her dress sense was immaculate, more in line with that of an accountant out to impress than a police officer.

'No, nothing. The body was out of the sight of the security office, suggesting whoever dumped the body knew the security guard's routine.'

'Do we know how long had it been there?' the same voice asked.

'First indications suggest he was killed at around 3 a.m., so we have a window of between then and 6.15 a.m. As I said, the time isn't precise.'

'Do we have any idea who he is?'

'The SOCO found a mobile phone, car keys and wallet in the victim's jacket.' Gowan turned towards DS Bright. 'Jenny, was there anything in it to give us a clue?'

'There were a couple till receipts from the Asda on Kingswood - one from the store and the other was from the petrol station - credit and debit card and a driving licence all in the same name of Thomas Gleeson. Lee's running his details through the database now.'

'Any address?' asked Marlowe.

'Yes, sir, according to the driving licence, he lived in the Beverley Road area.'

Marlowe moved back towards the centre of the room, looking around at the team. 'As I have already said, we've bugger-all to go on at this stage. With a bit of luck, Lee should be able to tell us a little more about him.'

As if appearing by magic, Lee entered the squad room with a folder in his hand as Marlowe finished.

'Find anything useful?'

'A fair bit, sir. Gleeson's not known to us on a local level, but when I ran his name through the PNC database, a bit more came to light. He's originally from Leeds, born and bred. He lived there until eighteen months ago when he went missing. Must have been keeping his head down.'

'Form?' Marlowe tried to stifle a yawn.

'The usual sort of stuff. Started when he was a kid, shoplifting, then progressed onto mugging, bag snatching, that sort of thing. As he got a bit older, he eventually moved on to the heavier stuff, dealing mainly, with a little GBH and pimping thrown in. He did time in a young offenders' unit and six months in Leeds nick for supplying. He's been out for two years and, on the surface, he has been as clean as a whistle since then. I had a word with the liaison officer at Leeds Metropolitan and he told me he could be a nasty sod if you got on the wrong side of him. He had delusions above himself, a hankering for the big time. He just seemed to disappear off their radar, so they wondered where he'd show up. Glad to see the back of him, he said.'

The young TDC closed up his folder and moved to the back of the room, leaving centre stage to the DCI

'Ok, then, Lee's put a bit more meat on the bone. Let's get to it.' Marlowe walked across to the DI Gowan. 'Dave, get them sorted. I'll tell the Super where we're at. Come to the office when you're done and get everybody back here for 4.30 p.m. for a briefing.'

Marlowe picked up his papers, looked around the room and left to go to his own office, grabbing a coffee from the machine on his way.

* * *

The computer screen, as ever, flickered with emails waiting to be read or ignored. Marlowe put the plastic coffee cup to one side of the desk and slumped down wearily. He rested his head back on his chair, took off his spectacles and rubbed his eyes with the back of his hands, then ran a hand through his short cropped grey hair. He was feeling distinctly weary after his early start. He picked up his coffee and allowed himself a moment or two before he rang the Superintendent with an update. *Bugger it*, he thought, opened his desk drawer and took out a packet of Bensons. Walking across to the office window, which faced out onto the car park, he stuck his head through it to check the coast was clear.

Good, he thought, and lit up.

* * *

DI Gowan sat on the edge of his desk. 'Right, let's get to it. Jenny, get down to Beverley Road and check out Gleeson's address, ask the neighbours about him, see what you can find out, the usual stuff, and take Tanya with you.'

DS Bright nodded.

'Lee, I want you to start checking any CCTV footage of the river side quay area. Start at about 2 a.m. until the time the body was found, and don't forget the Asda cameras, and

24

those in between. The rest of you check out your informants, see if anybody knows this bloke. Somebody must know him.'

The DI walked across to DC Lawson. 'Jonno, get down to Pride Security and see if you can get a print out of last nights shifts and then check out the security guy that found him.'

'No problem. On my way,' replied DC Jonno Lawson, the oldest and one of the most experienced members of the squad.

One by one, Gowan watched them filter out of the office. He spent a couple of minutes gathering his thoughts, then, armed with a coffee and what information they had, he knocked on the DCI's door and went in. Marlowe and Gowan had worked together for the past three years and had come to know each other over that time, good and bad for both of them.

'Sit down, Dave,' said Marlowe. 'I've just been on with the Super and, to be honest, we don't have a lot of time. He's didn't set a time limit as yet, but if we don't make any significant progress quickly, he's passing it onto Central. Is everything sorted out there?'

Gowan placed his coffee on the desk and sat down opposite the DCI. 'Yeah, all got jobs; I've been going through Gleeson's mobile. I think you might be interested to know that he had the Barnes brothers listed.'

'Well I never, that's something I wasn't expecting. We can't be that lucky this early in the investigation. Mind you, it's not their usual MO.'

'I know what you mean. It's a bit heavy, even for them. I'll go and have a word with the Brothers Grimm, see what they have to say.' Gowan stood ready to leave.

Marlowe smiled for the first time that day. 'I can't miss this, I know it's probably a waste of time, but I'll come with you. Just give me a few minutes to get sorted.'

DS Jenny Bright and DC Tanya Etherington signed out one of the pool cars, a blue Ford Focus.

'Look at the state of this. You wouldn't think it was a new car,' grumbled Tanya. 'Don't they ever get cleaned out? It's disgusting.' Paper cups and empty crisp packets littered the foot well. Tanya picked up the rubbish, threw it into the back and brushed away the crisp crumbs before sitting in the driving seat. 'Right, Sarge, what's the address on Beverley Road?'

Jenny fastened the passenger seat belt, 'Dewsbury Street. It's on the left just after the railway crossing, number twenty six.'

Tanya had joined the police straight from college at eighteen and served three years in Uniform before coming into CID. After a further year in CID at a rural station, she had become restless and had recently transferred from the market town of Driffield to Hull, with the hope of gaining more experience in a city force and looking forward to the excitement she hoped would come with the job.

'Is this your first murder case?' DS Bright asked.

'When I was in Uniform I was involved in one or two, a pub stabbing and a burglary that went wrong, but not directly involved like this.' DC Etherington put on her seat belt. 'How long have you been working with the Boss?' she asked as she put the car into gear and pulled out of the nick car park.

'About eighteen months. I came from Priory when my promotion came through,' replied Jenny. 'He's ok. Easy-going to a degree, but he can be a bloody single-minded sod when he wants.'

It had stopped raining by the time Jenny and Tanya left Gordon Street. They turned left down the Boulevard and headed along Selby Street towards the Anlaby Road, passing under the flyover and close to the Kingston Communications Stadium, home to the city's recently relegated Premier League football team, Hull City AFC. Tanya took a left onto the Anlaby Road, then another left at the light at the Park Street traffic lights, doing her best to avoid the town centre.

She cursed as they drove. There seemed to be road works on every corner. The pavements were full with jostling housewives and young single mothers pushing buggies, many of whom barely looked old enough to have children. Hull had the worst under-age pregnancy rate in the country.

She eased the car into a gap between a Mondeo and a Skoda outside of 26 Dewsbury Street, a red brick mid-terraced house with a drab exterior of worn wood and flaking paintwork.

There was no garden and the front door faced straight onto the pavement. Jenny noticed that all the curtains were closed, upstairs and downstairs.

The two detectives walked across the pavement to the front door and Tanya knocked loudly on the glass panel. They waited patiently for an answer, but none came.

'Tanya, go around the back and have a look.'

Tanya nodded and walked two houses further down the street, disappearing down a passage between the houses, which was littered with pizza boxes, fish and chip papers and rotting rubbish. The smell of cat pee was overpowering. The bottom of the passage was a block-end.

She turned left and back on herself until she came to the wooden door leading into the back yard of number 26. The yard door was unlocked but stiff. She put her shoulder against it, pushed hard, the door gave way to find yet more rubbish. She kicked the crap aside and tried the house door.

Jenny took Gleeson's keys from her coat pocket and tried them one by one. Third time lucky and the lock clicked. She turned the handle. The door opened leading straight into the living room.

The DS was surprised at how tidy the room was. Her eyes scanned the floor carefully as she made her through to the small kitchen at the rear of the house where she slipped the Yale latch on the back door and let Tanya in.

'Well, he might have been a bit of a scroat but he liked to keep a tidy house. Shame about the back way. It stinks of cat pee out there,' the DC remarked as she stepped into the kitchen. Like the living room, the kitchen was immaculately clean, a place for everything barring a few dirty pots on the sink unit drainer.

Directly off the kitchen the steep dogleg stairs led to the two bedrooms and bathroom on the next floor.

'Ok, Tanya, you go and have a look around upstairs and I'll start in here.'

At the top of the staircase, directly opposite, was the small bathroom. Tanya donned a pair of latex gloves and stepped in.

The bathroom was like the downstairs rooms - clean, compact, and tidy with a white suite. The only storage was a small plastic wall cupboard with mirror doors containing his toothbrush, shampoo and washing things.

The small bedroom, which overlooked the back yard, didn't look as if it was in use. A small single unmade bed was pushed against the longest wall and storage boxes were lined up against the other containing too much stuff for Tanya to sort through, so she thought it best to have them checked out later.

She closed the door and crossed the landing to the main bedroom. The curtains were still drawn. She left them shut and switched on the light.

The double bed was still made up and appeared not to have been slept in. A pair of dirty socks and a tee shirt lay on top. On either side of the bed were low pine cabinets. On one, a Stephen King novel lay upside down, keeping its place next to the reading lamp. A clock, aftershave and a half-full ashtray sat on the other. In the matching pine wardrobe, the clothes hung neatly on hangers - trousers, shirts and a suit, with three pairs of shoes lined up below, polished, of course.

The DC searched the suit pockets, but found nothing of any interest. Equally, she found nothing but socks, underwear and t-shirts in the top two drawers of the dresser.

The bottom drawer contained all his personal paperwork. This she put in a large plastic evidence bag to take back to the station when they left.

DS Bright was busy giving the kitchen a once over. On the long worktop were three storage jars for tea, coffee and sugar. The DS stirred about in the sugar and coffee, then tipped the tea bags onto the unit top and shouted to Tanya. 'Hey, come and have a look at this.' Amongst the tea bags were twelve small plastic packets with white powder inside.

'He might have been tidy but he can't have been all that bright. In amongst the tea bags!' Tanya took a plastic evidence bag from her jacket pocket and passed it to the DS who placed the suspect packages into the bag and sealed it.

'No prizes for guessing what's in them,' Jenny said. 'Any good upstairs?'

'No, clean as a whistle up there. A lot of storage boxes in the back bedroom that'll need to be checked out. This bloke seems to have been a tidy freak.'

'You can say that again. I could have done with him around my place for a couple of hours a week. Let's take a look around the living room.'

A television and DVD player occupied one corner and an armchair another. A coffee table was placed in front of a sofa facing the wall-mounted gas fire. On top of the coffee table was the previous evening's Hull Daily Mail, a car magazine and a laptop computer still charging from the mains electricity. Everything seemed impersonal.

As the two detectives prepared to leave the property, Tanya picked up the laptop. 'I don't suppose we will find much on this, but you never know,' she said as they walked into the street, locking the door behind them.

'When we get back, I'll have a word with Brice and ask him to send Forensics down to go through the place. Better get Uniform to do a door-to-door while we're at it,' said Jenny

* * *

'We'll take my car.' Marlowe said as they walked into the car park. 'How's it going, Dave, and I don't mean work?'

DI Gowan was the latest of the many police force divorce statistics - too many late nights and too much drink, like many before him.

'Not too bad, Joan lets me see the kids pretty much when I want. Mind you, it isn't as often as I would like.'

'Are they still at Joan's mothers?'

'Yeah, got to get the timing right to avoid the old bag. They're still there for the time being. She's had a look at a couple of flats, but hasn't found anything suitable for the kids. I told her if things aren't working out at the old bag's, I'll move out of the house and they can come back. But you know what she's like; got to do things her way.'

'Yeah, well, I was lucky in that respect with not having kids.' And besides, he thought, let her and Shag Pile Charlie the carpet salesman get on with it.

The DCI concentrated on the heavy traffic along the Anlaby Road before turning down Walton Street and past the entrance to the KC Stadium. The traffic was quite light during the week, unlike on Saturday when City was playing at home.

* * *

The Barnes brothers lived on the Copse Mead Estate; an estate they'd grown up on and controlled since they were kids. Now as adults, their reach went much further into the city, and beyond - drugs, protection, prostitution and the occasional gun. If there was money to be made, they would be involved at some stage.

The Copse Mead was built on the extreme northern edge of the city Kingston upon Hull, known to the locals simply as 'ull. The estate had been the planner's idea of sixties utopia with sprawling acres of prefabricated pebble-dashed houses and tower blocks. Rat runs abounded, aided by dingy subways, and meaningless expanses of municipal grass between the blocks isolated the people further. This was supposed to solve Hull's chronic housing problem when the West Hull slum clearance took place. What the do-gooders didn't take into account were the people they sent there; they alienated families and uprooted thousands of residents. In reality the council did very little for the tight knit communities they forced into migration; the community spirit disappeared never to return.

Gary Barnes liked to think he was a class above the others on the Copse Mead with his designer clothes and lifestyle. Home was a top floor flat in one of the tower blocks. The flat had more in common with an exclusive apartment development than a council tower block. The long picture window faced south-west with a fantastic view over the city and across the River Humber. The large expanse of glass captured the best of the sunlight, which spread year round warmth around the place. Gary's "penthouse" was furnished with luxury carpets, a fifty inch

32

plasma television on the wall and fitted out with very, very expensive furniture. His was the only block of flats where the stairwell didn't smell of urine and didn't have needles on the stairs, and the lift actually worked. In contrast, brother Pete, living on the same estate, called home a grubby three bedroomed semi. Without doubt the place was expensively fitted out, but much misused, as was Pete himself.

Marlowe enjoyed an outing, preferable to being tied to a desk. It was unusual for an officer of DCI rank to be involved in front-end policing, but over the years, Marlowe had managed to piss off more than a couple of his superior officers and was just left to get on with it. The DCI believed the higher-ups thought of it as banishment, but Marlowe quite enjoyed working out of Gordon Street.

After a short journey to the North of the city, Marlowe pulled the Mondeo into the kerb edge outside Pete Barnes' semi on the Copse Mead Estate. From the outside, it looked tidy enough with its small front garden boxed in with a wooden fence. Marlowe made sure the car was locked. No point taking risks. After all, they were on the Copse Mead.

They crossed the grass verge, avoiding the dog shit. Gowan gave the rickety gate that was hanging on one rusty hinge a push. The DI rang the front door bell, keeping his finger pressed down. He did this several times and then hammered on the door with his fist and waited, but there was no answer. He peered through the front window but it was obvious no one was at home.

'Looks like we've missed out on this one, Boss. What about Gary's place?'

33

'Ok, we might as well give it a try,' Marlowe agreed as they headed back down the path to the car for the five minute drive to the other side of the estate.

They took the non piss-smelling, graffiti free lift to the thirteenth floor, Gary Barnes' flat was directly opposite the lift entrance and had been fitted with a steel-plated door, complete with spy hole.

The lift doors closed behind them and the motor started returning the metal box to ground level.

DI Gowan hammered on the door and rang the bell, no response. Marlowe thought it more than likely they'd been spotted driving up and no one was answering. They waited a short while until it was obvious no one was going to answer the door.

'Well, this has been a waste of bloody time,' said Marlowe as he turned back towards the lift and pressed the call button. 'Let's get back to the nick, get Uniform to keep an eye on the estate and have them picked up when they show.'

Chapter 3

By the time Marlowe and Gowan had returned to the station, it was just after 4.30 p.m. and the rest of the team was already assembled. The chattering stopped as they walked into the room.

Gowan went and sat at his desk while Marlowe walked to the front of the squad room, contemplating whilst looking at the latest pictures on the whiteboard.

'Ok,' Marlowe turned to face the team. 'What have we got?' He looked around the room at the pensive faces. 'You first,' he said, nodding his head towards trainee detective Kristianson.

'The only actual sighting we have of the victim is at the petrol station on the Kingswood 'Asda' site. Security cameras clocked him at 8.17 p.m. last night when he filled up. Looks like he was driving a light coloured Astra. We got a registration from the camera and the follow up with the DVLA confirmed it does, or did, belong to the victim.'

'What about the cameras on and around the quay?'

'Not much at all,' answered Kristianson. 'I checked out the footage from 2.00 am. until the time the body was found. The cameras actually on the quay are very few and far between, and the ones that do work are in pretty crap locations, just dark and grainy images not worth anything.

There was one thing that was out of place. Around 4.00 a.m. this morning, what looks like a dark coloured Ford Transit Connect went onto the quay and left again eight minutes later. The only identification on the vehicle was the last two letters painted on the side: something A, something... something... something A, something ER. Again, we only got a partial on the number plate: Y something ... something ... something S. This was from the only decent camera at the site entrance.'

'That's a lot of somethings,' quipped the DI.

'Yeah, I know. The camera situation down there really is crap.'

'Is this a time when the security guard is on patrol?' DI Gowan asked.

'No, I checked it out with Pride. It coincides with the times the security officer should be in the office. Could be just a coincidence.'

'I don't like coincidences. More like he might know the quay and security routine.' Marlowe turned to Jenny and Tanya. 'Did you two find anything in his house?'

'A dozen wraps of white powder concealed under the tea bags. Pretty obvious what's in them, Forensic is checking them out anyway. Apart from that, it was clean.'

'We picked up his laptop and sent it to technical. You never know,' added Tanya. 'We have a couple of PCs doing house-to-house enquiries,' she added as an afterthought.

Marlowe moved towards the window and stared across the car park thoughtfully, then turned back to face the team. 'Jonno, did you turn up anything on the security guard?'

Jonno picked up his notebook, flicked it open and addressed the team. 'Clean as a whistle. Twelve years in the Royal Air Force Regiment, commended twice and joined Pride Security when he came out. Well thought of by the management, a very conscientious bloke, been with them three years now. Married with two kids, lives on Hessle Road down Corsair Close, and that's it.'

Marlowe looked at his watch and decided to call time. 'OK, it's been a long day and we've had a bad start. Let's see what tomorrow brings. See you all in the morning, bright and early.'

Marlowe returned to his office to try and concentrate on the endless paperwork. Half an hour later, he was surprised when he lifted his head as the DI knocked and walked in. 'You still here, Dave?'

'Yeah, just off. I'm going for a pint if you fancy one.'

'No thanks, Dave I'm knackered, I'll pass. I'm going to pick up a takeaway on the way home. See you tomorrow.'

It had been a long day. By the time Marlowe decided to go home, the rest of the team were probably on their second pint.

* * *

DCI Philip Marlowe lived in the nearby market town of Beverley, eight miles north of Hull. Home was a narrow boat moored on a stretch of water near the lock head on the Beverley Beck, which had been his home for the last two years since his wife had run off with Shag Pile Charlie. He'd seen it coming for a long time, but had done bugger all about it. Like Dave, too many late nights, too much drinking and too many broken promises.

"You're never bloody here," she'd told him.

He couldn't argue with that.

"You're married to the job," she'd told him.

Well, yes, but not in the biblical sense.

"You love that bloody mongrel more than me," she'd told him.

Yes, that was definitely true.

When he did think about it, she was absolutely right, it had been inevitable and he'd done bugger all to try and stop it. The only thing he had left to remind him of fifteen years of marriage was Archie, a three year old black and white mongrel of questionable parentage, a strange looking dog with short legs, a biggish body and long drooping ears.

Marlowe drove down the towpath to the secure compound which housed the residential boats. He pulled up at the gates, eased himself out of the car, unlocked the gates and grimaced as his back twinged when he eased himself back into the vehicle. He parked the Mondeo and locked the compound gates behind him.

The Daisy was seventy feet in length, seven feet across the beam and painted in the traditional bright colours - red, shades of blue and yellow - not that it looked very appealing in the winter gloom. Moored up to two concrete bollards, the Daisy, along with the other residential boats, was connected up to all the land-based services.

Marlowe walked across the short gangway and unlocked the hatch, before climbing down the three steps into the small but fully equipped galley. Every nook and cranny had been filled with cupboards, drawers and mini electrical appliances.

38

Archie, the DCI's four-legged friend, had heard the Mondeo pulling into the compound and was sitting at the galley hatch, furiously wagging his tail. Marlowe took off his damp outside jacket and hung it next to the solid fuel boiler. He bent over and fussed the dog for a couple of minutes, then reached into one of the low cupboards for the dog's food. He opened a tin of Chum and scooped half of it into Archie's bowl, and watched as his canine friend quickly devoured his evening meal.

Marlowe rinsed his hands under the tap, took a plate out of the cupboard, tipped the takeaway of prawn curry he'd collected on his way home onto it, and put it in the microwave. He seemed to be surviving on convenience food these days.

He took off his tie, kicked off his shoes and put on his slippers, before taking a bottle of red wine from the rack. Fine wine was Marlowe's second vice after the cigarettes, and he liked to think he was a bit of a connoisseur when it came to a good wine.

The microwave purred as he poured himself a large Cabernet Sauvignon. The deep ruby liquid swirled in his glass, just like in a Marks and Spencer's advertisement. When the microwave pinged, he picked up a knife and fork, carried his meal, along with his wine, through to the saloon, and settled back on the sprung cushions of the corner dinette. With the empty plate on the table in front of him, he refilled his glass, picked up the stereo remote and clicked. Melancholy music filled the small saloon.

He had just about finished the bottle of red before his eyes started to close and he fell into a deep sleep with the dog on the cushion next to him.

He stayed there all night until 6.30 a.m., not even waking for a piss, and that was strange.

'Bloody hell. Again?' he said aloud as he tried to stretch out his aching back and neck. Unfortunately, sleeping on the dinette was a bad habit he had recently developed.

Marlowe moved into the galley, filled the kettle, turned it on, and went into the bedroom to strip off his clothes. In comparison to the saloon, the double bedroom was quite large. Once undressed, he climbed into the en suite shower cubicle. His body tingled as the cold water turned to hot and ran down his face and body, putting life back into his limbs after the night on the dinette.

Feeling refreshed, he towelled himself dry, shaved and dressed, and went back to the galley. He dropped a tea bag in a mug and poured the boiling water over it. Armed with his mug of tea, he sat once more at the dinette, tuned the radio to Radio Humberside, the local station, and wasn't surprised to hear mention of the previous day's murder.

> *"Police are investigating the suspicious death of a man found on the riverside quay..."*

At least they didn't have all the gruesome details.

Before leaving the Daisy, Marlowe gave Archie the remainder of the food from the tin and took him onto the towpath for a quick constitutional before securing him in his run in the compound. He shivered when he went up on deck. Overnight the weather had taken a distinct turn. The wind was blowing from the north, bringing with it a bright blue sky and a penetrating cold.

If it had not been for the old couple, Joyce and Harry, who lived in the old lock keeper's cottage, caring for the dog during the day, keeping Archie would have been out of the question. Harry, a retired sheet metal worker, liked to keep himself active and did any odd jobs that needed doing on board the Daisy. He always came for Archie at breakfast time and looked after him until evening, taking him for long walks along the towpath, which they both enjoyed, and then, depending on the weather, returning him to the pen in time for Marlowe's arrival back from work.

By 7.30 a.m., Archie was secured in his pen and DCI Philip Marlowe was back in the Mondeo driving down the A1174, heading for the Gordon Street Nick.

Chapter 4

Dave Gowan looked his usual self - rough. Although tall and slim, he didn't carry his clothes well. He was the sort of man you could put in an Armani suit and he would still look like he had had a makeover in a charity shop.

Today was the exception; he looked worse.

'You look knackered,' Jenny told Dave as they sat over an early morning coffee in the station canteen. 'Rough night, was it?' she added with a smirk.

'You could say that. Stopped for a pint in the George on the way home. Big mistake. I got talking to some old gadger who used to work on the trawlers. He said he went to sea straight from school as a deckie learner and ended up a skipper. Well, you know what it's like with these old blokes, story after story. Next thing I knew, the landlord called time. Had to get a taxi as I was half pissed, and a bit more,' the DI sniggered.

'So that's the reason there's no big greasy fry up in front of you and your eyes look like piss holes in the snow.'

'Please don't talk about it. I can't face food just yet.' He held his stomach and grimaced as he spoke. 'How about you? Get up to anything?'

'Me? What do you think? The same as usual - home, dinner, bath, book and bed. That seems to be about it these days.'

'Yeah, I know what you mean. You don't get much time to develop a social life in this job.'

'Talking about not feeling very well, have you heard any more about Karl? He's been off quite a while now.' Jenny pushed her coffee cup into the centre of the table.

'I haven't seen hide nor hair of him since he went sick again. One of the traffic lads said they spoke to him a couple of months back. He hardly recognised the poor bugger. Looks a right mess, apparently. He's really let himself go.'

'That's what grief does to you. Mind you, I did think the PI would have sorted out a replacement DS by now. It's a bit much working a man down. As I've said, it does no good for my love life.' Jenny stuffed her belongings into her bag and deliberately pushed back her chair, making a squealing noise as the legs scraped along the floor tiles. The DI's face screwed up at the noise. It wasn't exactly the right sound to accompany his hangover. 'Come on. The PI will be in soon,' Jenny said as they both collected their belongings and headed for the squad room.

'Got any aspirins?' Dave asked as they left. Jenny shook her head.

They started down the stairwell from the first floor canteen. Sergeant Cleeves was coming towards them, huffing and puffing with the exertion. He stopped two steps below them and bent over, resting his hands on his knees, stopping them in their tracks by waving a file above his head.

43

'Is – is – the PI in yet?' he puffed and panted between breaths, looking more than a bit red in the face.

'Haven't seen him yet,' replied Gowan.

'Right,' mumbled the sergeant as he regained his breath. 'Give him this when he comes in. There's been another two off-licences knocked off last night.' Cleeves passed over the folder and made his way back down the stairs to the custody area.

'Watch your blood pressure, Trev. We don't want you keeling over,' the DI called after him.

'Piss off,' he managed to blow out.

* * *

The sergeant eventually got his breath back and was busy behind the custody desk with his head down, studying the morning reports, as Marlowe stepped into the reception from the car park. He smiled as he looked up. As usual, he couldn't resist it. 'Of all the nicks in all the world...'

Marlowe cut him short before he had time to finish. 'That's Bogart, you silly bugger,' he snapped as he headed for the CID office, holding up a two fingered salute.

'Passed a file to Gowan for you.' Cleeves called after him.

Marlowe kept walking and waved his hand in the air in acknowledgement.

* * *

The team were already in the CID office and talking over last night's exploits of who'd seen what on the television. For some reason Coronation Street seemed to be the favourite topic of the morning. It was usually Emmerdale. Nobody in the office seemed to like Eastenders.

44

Lee sat at his desk with his chair slightly facing towards the corridor. 'Hey up, the gaffer's coming,' he said with pen in hand, putting his head down and trying to look busy.

'Morning all,' greeted Marlowe as he walked into the squad room to the welcome of early morning grunts and groans. 'Glad to see you're all fit and raring to go. Briefing in ten minutes,' he added as he purposely slammed the door into the frame behind him to wake them up.

Once in his office, he took off his wax jacket and hung it on the rack. Next, he turned on the coffee machine without bothering to check it; the Pyrex jug was still half full of yesterday's congealed brew. Once he was settled behind his desk, he decided he'd better try and have a quick catch-up on his paperwork, reading through the statements, audits, appraisals, court appearances and other miscellaneous stuff that went with the job of being a DCI. He sighed to himself when he saw the screen full of emails, one in particular grabbed his attention: a message, or perhaps more of an order, from the superintendent asking for an update on the murder inquiry. This was not a task he was looking forward to. Marlowe had known the uniformed superintendent for a number of years and they had never really got on.

Twenty minutes later, the Marlowe entered the squad room. He glanced around before sitting on the corner of the nearest desk, which belonged to DC Jonno Lawson. 'Right, anything come in overnight?' he asked no one in particular.

'A uniformed patrol found Gleeson's Astra last night.' The voice belonged to DC Tanya Etherington.

'Where did they find it?'

'Not far away, on Hessle Road, parked up down Constable Street, near the Criterion pub. Apparently it had been there a couple of days, but nobody thought anything about it. A patrol car came across it and did a routine check.'

'OK, Tanya, that's you sorted out. Follow it up. With a bit of luck we might find some evidence to link it in with the Brothers Grimm.' Marlowe waited for the next response.

'Still no sign of the Barnes brothers,' chipped in Dave Gowan. 'Told uniform to keep a keen eye out and pick them up first chance they get.'

Marlowe turned towards DS Bright. 'Did anything come up from the door-to-door enquiries?'

'Nothing to speak of, Boss. Half of the people down the street didn't know him. Those that did say he was a quiet bloke who kept himself to himself. The old lady directly opposite on the other side is a bit of an insomniac. Sits up half the night looking out of the window. Said he came and went at odd hours, day and night. She didn't know if he had a job or not,' said Jenny, reading from her notes.

'OK, thanks, Jenny. See if you can chase up the post-mortem results.' Marlowe stood up, brushed down the creases in his trousers and put his hands in his pockets. 'Jonno, have a word with your informers. See if anybody knew him. That's it, then, everyone. Let's get to work.'

* * *

Dave Gowan stood in front of Marlowe's desk and passed across the folder.

'Trev gave this to me. Two more off-licences done over last night.'

Marlowe took the report from him and scanned through it.

'Doesn't look too taxing. Give it to Lee and see what he can do. Can't do any harm. I'd like you to have another word down at Pride Security. Out of everyone, they should know what's happening on the quay.'

'Yeah, they must have some sort of a list of what businesses are down there. With a bit of luck they might keep a log of vehicles entering and leaving. If that's the case, we might get an early result.'

The conversation carried on for a further ten minutes as they discussed the other cases the department was involved with. Once the day-to-day stuff was organised, Gowan returned to the squad room. 'Right, I'm going to Pride and then down the quay. If I'm needed, get me on the mobile,' he called to no one in particular as he took his coat off the rack and headed for the door.

* * *

Marlowe was staring at the computer screen, deleting countless spam emails that had come through overnight, offering mail order Viagra and penis enlargement.

DS Bright knocked on the door and walked in. The DCI looked up and motioned for Jenny to take the vacant seat opposite.

'Preliminary report on the post mortem has just come in,' she said, waving a file in the air.

'Good. Have you had time to have a look at it?' asked Marlowe as he looked up over the top of his spectacles.

'A brief glance. Haven't had time to study it yet.'

'That's ok. Give me the quick version.'

47

'The initial findings are just as Brice thought. The nail through the scull penetrated the brain, causing death instantaneously. He had a fair amount of old bruising around the body and a couple or ribs that hadn't healed from what could have been a kicking. The nail is not the only interesting thing; toxicology showed a fair amount of alcohol and a large amount of heroin in his system. If the nail hadn't killed him, the heroin would have. Even stranger, there was also a trace of Rohypnol, the date rape drug, in his system.'

This grabbed the DCI's attention. 'Bloody hell, that as well as the nail job? Whoever did it definitely meant business. Have Forensic come up with anything significant about the nail?'

'You must be kidding. You can buy the same type from B&Q, Focus or any other DIY store in the country - bog standard four inch wire nail. It's the same with the remnants of the parcel tape, you can buy it anywhere.'

'Don't suppose there is any prints either?'

Jenny didn't have to look at her notes for the answer to the question. 'Yes and no. Plenty, but it will take a while to have them checked out on the system and we're still waiting for any DNA results.'

'What about his house?'

'SOCO did have a bit better luck at the house. Underneath the sink unit, taped to the back of the bowl, they found seven hundred and fifty quid in notes, along with a half a pound of coke in a plastic bag.'

'That's a lot of stuff for a small time-dealer. Bit different to the usual toilet cistern. Shows some initiative,' Marlowe said smiling. 'So, in the meantime, we've still bugger all to go on until the results come in.' He took off his spectacles and cleaned them with his tie. 'Let me know if they get anything, and see if Forensic found anything in the car,' Marlowe said, putting his spectacles back on. 'And keep an eye on Lee. He's looking into the off-licence break-ins. He shouldn't get into too much bother.'

There was a sardonic edge to his voice.

* * *

DI Gowan was just pulling up at the Pride Security office when his mobile came to life. Leaving the phone in the hands-free kit, he hit the answer key. 'Gowan.'

'Dave, it's Phil. We're going for a pint. I'll see you outside the Criterion about twelve o'clock. I might even buy you lunch.'

The Pride Security office was on the Livingstone Business Park. It was a very professional looking company from the outside, with high galvanized steel fencing surrounding the building and a gravelled parking area to the front. The DI was even more impressed when he walked through the plate glass doors into the ultra-modern interior with its chrome and glass furniture, and potted plants. Framed photographs of some of their prestigious customers' buildings were placed artistically on the walls.

A smartly dressed young woman with a pleasant face occupied the reception desk. Gowan gave her his best smile.

'Good morning. How may I help?'

'Morning, I'm Detective Inspector Gowan, I'd like to speak with someone regarding the incident on the quay.'

'If you would like to take a seat for a moment, I'll fetch someone,' she said, gesturing him to the seating area.

Gowan sat on one of the tubular chrome chairs, studied the palatial surroundings and picked up a magazine. After a short wait of a couple of minutes, a tall, well-built middle-aged man with a red face and receding hairline came into the reception area and introduced himself as the contracts manager.

'How can I help?' he asked, holding out his hand to the DI.

'Morning.' Gowan dropped the magazine to the table and reached out to shake hands. 'I'm Detective Inspector Gowan, and you are?'

'Sorry, Chris York. What can I do for you, Inspector?'

'It's about the body your guy found on Monday morning. I was hoping you might be able to furnish us with any information you might have.'

'Like what, specifically?'

'Anything, really. Has anything happened out of the ordinary, any new contractors working on the quay, that sort of thing?'

'No, not really. We don't actually monitor the quay for its day-to-day activities. There's people coming and going all the time. Speaking for ourselves, we've had the computer people down there, and the only regular outside people we have on the quay are our two-way radio contractors. Our repeater station is down there.'

'Have they been with you long?' asked Gown.

'Both companies have, since we started up about seven years ago. The computer people are from Selby and a local

50

company down Park Street looks after the radio kit. I'll get their details for you.'

'You can't remember anyone else - no emergency work?'

'No, none that I am aware of, but I will double check. What with the credit crunch and cut backs, most of the businesses down there are in the same boat as us, putting things on hold.'

'I'd appreciate it if you could give me a list of all the companies on the quay before I go.'

'No problem. I'll get it for you.' The contracts manager leaned towards the girl on the reception desk and said something. She disappeared into a side room. Two minutes later, she returned with a list that she passed to the DI.

'If you do remember anything, I'd appreciate it if you would give me a call.' The DI passed across his business card and said his thanks. Feeling disgruntled at having drawn another blank, Gowan decided to try his luck on the quay. *Somebody must know something*, he thought.

By the time he had travelled back along Hessle Road to the crime scene, it was fully light - as light as it was going to get, anyway. He could see the forensic team and the search section were still on the scene. The tarpaulins that had been erected on Monday morning had been replaced with a more substantial tent to preserve the area, even though the victim had long been removed to the mortuary.

Gowan parked his car as near to the scene as possible, went around the back of the car, popped the boot lid and took out a hi-visibility waterproof jacket. This time he was more prepared and suitably dressed to face the rain that again had started to blow across the Humber.

51

'How's it going, George?' he called out to the dripping wet uniformed sergeant in charge of the search team.

'Not very well at the minute, Dave. The lads have started to widen the search area, but what with this bloody weather, I don't suppose we'll get bugger all worth having that we didn't find yesterday.'

'Cheers. Let me know if you do find anything.'

Feeling even more pissed off and miserable, Gowan pulled the hood of his police jacket over his already dripping hair and started to trawl the workshops.

The telephone rang the very second Marlowe put down the receiver.

'Marlowe,' he intoned into the handset, screwing up his face as he recognised the voice of Superintendent Bulmer. 'Ah, good morning, sir... Yes, I was meaning to give you an update. You know what it's like... No, we haven't got a suspect yet... Yes, I know it's been over twenty four hours ... Still early days...' Marlowe sat back in his chair listening to the droning voice go on. 'I can assure you, sir, we are making progress. Uniform found his car, and drugs have been found at his house... Yes, sir, I'll do that. As soon as we get something, you will be the first to know'. He hid his frustration and put the receiver down gently. He usually slammed the thing down after a call from the Super.

Prat, he thought.

Marlowe needed a post-Super caffeine fix. He pushed back his chair and flexed his leg muscles as he stood and walked across to his coffee machine. His mug could have done with a rinse, but he didn't bother and poured himself a cup of strong black liquid. He grimaced at the bitter taste when he realized it was heated up from the day before. He took the murky liquid back to his desk and started once again on the mountain of paperwork growing in his in- tray.

Chapter 5

The A1079 - Beverley Road - leading into the town, was the main route into the city from the North. The nearer you were to the city centre, the busier it became.

The area was fast becoming popular with Hull's ethnic community, especially the economic migrants from Eastern Europe. Ethnic coffee shops, Polish supermarkets and the like were opening up every hundred metres or so.

DC Jonno Lawson wasn't looking forward to the task of trekking up and down Beverley Road in the cold. Jonno was the same age as the DCI and, like the DCI, he'd been a long time in the job. Lawson was a persistent plodder and a competent copper who never wanted to be anything other than be a DC. He loved the job, but hated the thought of the stress that promotion would bring.

He parked the scratched and battered pool car in the Aldi supermarket car park next to a gleaming Beamer as tight as he could to the other vehicles driver's door, and smiled to himself; not that he was jealous or anything. He stepped over the low chain link fence out of the car park and onto the pavement to start his trek around the area, mingling in with the shoppers.

A young girl who looked to be no more than fifteen, dressed in pink tracksuit bottoms and a bright purple hoodie, came towards him, pushing an expensive-looking buggy; a few hundred quid's worth, he thought, probably bought for her offspring by the Social. Jonno was a father himself, but couldn't help staring at the overweight toddler in the buggy, its cheeks bulging, munching on a jumbo sausage roll.

'What?' The teenager challenged. 'Seen enough? You a perv or sommat?' She gave him a disgusted look as she pushed on. Jonno shook his head in disbelief. She had a gold ring in her nose and a pin through her eyebrow. The city was full of girls like this.

Time was getting on and by 11.30 a.m., he was on his third pub on Beverley Road. He'd already been in the Red Rose, the Station and the White Hart, and he still hadn't had any luck. He was freezing and desperate for the toilet by the time he reached the next one. The three glasses of lemon and lime were taking their effect on his bladder. He decided to have no more drinks as he dashed straight for a pee in the Whaler toilets.

He looked around as he came out of the toilet and could see no one except the big bloke behind the bar.

'Hiya, Charlie,' he called as he walked across to the landlord standing behind the highly polished dark coloured wooden bar.

'Morning, Jonno. I never saw you come in,' the landlord replied as he emptied a slop tray into a bucket.

'I went straight to the loo. I was busting.'

'Don't usually see you at this time of day. Must be official. Do you want a drink?'

'No, thanks. I've been pissing all morning. Do you recognise this bloke? No bugger else does.'

Lawson put a black and white photograph of the murdered man down on the bar top.

'Gleeson, Tom Gleeson.' the answer came back without hesitation. 'I've had to warn him off more than once for trying to sell shit.'

'Was he a regular?' asked Jonno.

'What do you mean *was?*'

'He's recently deceased.'

'I can't say I'll miss him. He started to come in on student nights when the special offers are on, but we soon got wise to him. We caught him a couple of times doing deals in the bogs. I had a word with the night door staff and had them warn him. It worked to some extent. It didn't stop him completely, though. He just went outside to do his deals, where the door staff couldn't see what was going on. Word is that he usually hung about around the pubs and clubs nearer the town centre during the week when the students are about, and then moved into the old town on a weekend.'

'Cheers, Charlie. I've been having trouble getting anybody to give me any info about him.'

'Well, can't blame them. You don't say much about the bloke you get your shit off, do you? You know the saying. "Don't crap on your own doorstep."'

'No, don't suppose you would. Thanks for your help, Charlie. Better get back to it.'

Lawson was reluctant to leave the warmth of the pub. He was just getting the feeling back in his toes. He buttoned up his overcoat, pulled the collar tight around his neck and nodded acknowledgement to the landlord.

'See you around.'

* * *

On the other side of the city, Hessle Road was once described as a "village within a city". This was at a time when the fishing industry was the economic staple of Hull. During the fifties and sixties, Hull had the largest fishing port in the world, but that was long ago.

The road was busy with shoppers. Even though the majority of traditional fish-related industries had gone, it still had a character all of its own. Many of the old public houses still existed – just - but now charity shops matched the number of regular businesses.

Marlowe turned the Mondeo left out of the Boulevard, heading for his meeting with the DI. The Criterion was only two streets further on. He parked the car in the small car park on the corner of Walcott Street, directly opposite the pub, and waited for Gowan.

The Criterion was one of those public houses that once thrived on the proceeds from the fishing industry. In the golden years, every public house along the road was full from the bar to the door with fishermen in their ice-blue coloured suits, with high waistband trousers and bell bottoms that completely covered their shoes and jackets, belted at the back. The fishermen would flash the cash like "weekend millionaires", deservedly so after three weeks at sea and with only forty-eight hours between trips.

Sitting in his car with the window down, smoking a Benson and Hedges, Marlowe was feeling a little nostalgic.

He could smell the fishy odour that carried in the wind off Albert Dock. He'd grown up not a spit away from where he sat waiting for the DI. For the best part of his early life, he'd been brought up in a "sham four", the local name for a terraced house with two rooms downstairs and two up. In those days there had been no hot water and the loo was outside, not forgetting the tin bath hung on a nail in the back yard. When he'd left school his first job had been as a barrow boy on the dock, shifting aluminium barrels, known as "kits", full of fish from place to place.

Before he had a chance to get too maudlin, Gowan drove up in a pool car. Marlowe lumbered out of the vehicle, locked it and flicked his cigarette end amongst the other rubbish as he walked over to meet him.

'How have you got on?' he asked immediately. 'Never mind, tell me over a pint.'

The two detectives waited for a gap in the traffic and dashed across the road to the pub opposite. Marlowe pushed open the frosted glass door and went over to the long mahogany bar. Over the bar was an impressive glass mirror with a picture of a trawler etched onto its surface.

'Afternoon, Officers,' acknowledged the barman.

'Bloody hell, is it that obvious?' Marlowe said as he put his foot on the brass rail and leant on the bar with his elbows.

'Intuition. When you've been in the business as long as I have, it becomes second nature.' The big man behind the bar touched the side of his nose and winked.

'What are you having? Marlowe asked the DI.

'Pint of lager please, Phil.' Using the DCI's Christian name was something Gowan would never do within earshot of his colleagues.

'Pint? Sure you don't want a half? We do have to go back to the station, you know.'

Dave gave him *piss off* look.

'Just kidding, and a glass of red, please,' Marlowe continued.

'Take a seat gents and I'll bring them over.'

The pub was still quite empty for a lunchtime. Two old chaps, complete with flat caps, sat in a corner playing dominoes and a group of men in overalls stood at the end of the bar having a liquid lunch. Marlowe walked over to a table near a frosted glass window and sat facing the door through force of habit.

The drinks appeared two minutes later. 'Cheers,' said the landlord as he set them down on the table.

'Let's order some food and you can fill me in on your morning.' The DCI picked up the menu, selected a shepherd's pie and passed the menu across to the DI.

'Hot pot sounds good. Yeah, I'll have the hot pot,' said Gowan.

Marlowe walked across to the bar and ordered the food. A few minutes later a smart young girl, who looked like she should still be at school, came from the kitchen and set cutlery down on the copper-topped table. She smiled politely and returned to the kitchen.

The two detectives talked about their various caseloads until the waitress returned with their meals, reaching across the table carefully as she placed their food down. 'Be careful. The plates are hot,' she warned.

'Thanks, love. This looks good. We're ready for it,' Marlowe said as he picked up his knife and fork. 'What's what, then, Dave?'

'Didn't come up with anything at the Pride security office. I had a word with their contracts manager. He told me they haven't had any builders or carpenters working on site for quite a while, what with the credit crunch and all that. The only regular contractors are their two radio people, a local company based down Park Street. I'll go and have a word later.'

Marlowe picked up his glass of wine and grimaced at the taste. The bitter vino wasn't quite what he was used to. 'Suppose there's a lot of companies like that just now. Can't blame them for hanging onto their cash with the state of things. Did you do any better on the quay?'

Gowan put down his knife and fork and picked up his pint of lager. 'Surprisingly so.' He wiped the lager top from his lips with the back of his hand. 'I spoke to a bloke who services air conditioning units. He remembered someone had a lock-up two units away from his. Apparently the bloke couldn't afford the rent and moved out around three weeks ago'.

'Did he know his name?'

'No such luck. He didn't speak to him much. Said he was a quiet bloke. One day he'd come and then he wouldn't see him for weeks. Not a friendly bloke. Said he'd just nod, then disappear into the workshop. Hardly spoke two words to him. Could have been a carpenter or anything, really.'

'The carpenter bit could fall in with the letters on the side of the van. Did he say what type of vehicle he drove?'

'This is the best bit,' said the DI. 'He remembered it was a dark blue Ford Transit Connect. He didn't know the reg, though.'

'It's about time we got a break on this one. It might get the bloody Super off my back.' Marlowe took out his wallet and pulled out a twenty as they both walked across to the bar to pay the bill. He then produced his ID and introduced himself and Dave to the barman.

'I'm DCI Marlowe and this is DI Gowan.'

Dave Gowan laid down a picture of the murder victim on the bar top. 'Don't suppose you have seen this man lately, have you?'

'Don't know him, but I think he might have been in on Sunday. That's right, he was in here Sunday night. Not a regular.' The barman walked across to the cash till with Marlowe's twenty pound note.

'Was he on his own?' asked the DCI.

'He was to start with. I only remember because we were pretty quiet. He looked as if he was half pissed and his mate had to help him out - not paralytic, just well oiled. I reckon he must have had a few before he came in here, though, 'cos he only had a couple of pints in here before they left.'

The barman brought back the change and put it down on the bar. Marlowe picked it up and slipped it into his pocket. 'Don't suppose you can tell us what his mate looked like.'

'Not really. I can only say he was older - about fifty at a guess. Tall bloke, around six foot, dark hair combed straight back, longish.'

'What about his clothes? Anything distinctive?' Gowan asked.

'Black jacket, blue jeans and trainers. That's it. Like I said, if the other bloke hadn't been the worse for wear I wouldn't have noticed either of them.'

Marlowe took out one of his business cards and passed it across to the barman. 'If you remember anything, or see the bloke again, I'd appreciate a call.'

'No problem, Officers. See you again.'

The barman slipped the card into his shirt pocket and went back to work wiping down the bar top as the two detectives walked towards the door.

Chapter 6

The traffic was chocker-block on Newland Avenue, a popular shopping area. TDC Kristianson could see the patrol car parked outside of the double-fronted off-licence sandwiched in between a ladies hairdressers and a charity shop. He pulled the pool car into the kerb edge and parked on double yellow lines directly behind the squad car.

'Oh shit,' Lee said out aloud, only to be given a filthy look by a little old lady as she passed. Kristianson smiled at her as he scraped the dog shit from his shoe along the kerb edge. He locked the car and crossed the pavement to the shop where the door was shut with the closed sign showing. He gave the door a shove and went in. Lee noticed the security grills were still down.

'Alright, Wayne, Terry?' Lee greeted his former uniform colleagues.

'Not bad, Lee. How are you getting on in a suit?' asked Wayne as he eyed him up and down, admiring the new suit. 'What's that smell? Not you, is it?'

Lee ignored the remark.

'Did your mam get you ready? You look like you've just come out of Matalan catalogue,' joked Terry.

Lee smiled at the good humoured banter then turned to Wayne. 'I'm good, thanks. What have you got?'

Wayne nodded his head for Lee to follow them behind the counter and through to the back of the premises.

'Come and have a look. Hardly brain surgery. They forced the back door, see.' Terry pointed to the back door, which from the state of it, had obviously been jemmied open with a crowbar. Wayne started to scribble in his notebook.

'Didn't the alarm go off?' asked Lee as he looked around the storeroom.

'Would you believe it, the alarm's not working. They've been waiting two days for an engineer to turn up. A couple coming home from the pub decided to have a quick grope around the back, noticed the door was open and called it in,' Wayne read from his notes.

'What about CCTV?'

'Good news on that one. It's working. The manager is setting the tape up now.'

The three of them went upstairs to the manager's office, struggling to get past the boxes that were stacked down one side.

'Bloody dangerous, this. If I worked here it would be a Health and Safety issue,' Terry muttered. Wayne was one of the few officers at Gordon Street who could put up with his perpetual moans and groans.

In his office, the manager hit the play button on the video recorder. 'Here we go, Officers.' The black and white picture flickered like an old-fashioned movie down to the time delay on the camera, and the pictures jumped slowly from frame to frame.

From over the manager's shoulder, Lee and the uniforms watched the crime unfold. It took around two minutes for the burglars to appear in the shop, both carrying crowbars and wearing ski masks. Once inside the shop the masks were discarded.

'Hang on. Stop it there. Rewind a bit, please,' instructed Wayne. 'I know that cheeky bugger.'

* * *

The private hire car turned left off Anlaby Road into Bean Street and pulled up outside a scruffy looking mid terraced house with a flaky blue painted wooden door.

Pete Barnes could see the grubby curtains were closed. He eased himself out into the street, leaving his brother, Gary, and the driver in the cab with the engine ticking over. This was their third stop that morning.

Pete gave the blue door a bang with his fist and walked straight in, shutting the door behind him. Five minutes later he came out of the house with a big grin on his face and a bulging envelope in his hand. Once back in the taxi, he passed it over to Gary. Gary flicked though the notes. 'Not bad, Pete,' he smiled at his brother as he put the package in his inside pocket. 'Another couple of collections like this and we'll be able to call it a day. I love it when a plan comes together,' he said using his best "A Team" voice.

An hour later the taxi pulled up outside Pete's semi on the Copse Mead. After making arrangements to meet later that evening, Pete climbed out of the cab, kicked the garden gate open and walked down the path to his front door. As the cab pulled away, Gary on instinct turned and looked behind just as two uniformed police officers approached from around the corner. 'Fuckers,' he said aloud. It was pretty obvious they had been keeping a watch on the house. There was bugger all he could do about it; Gary knew he'd be next to be picked up. He leaned forward to the driver and told him to take him back into the city and drop him off in the city centre.

* * *

The taxi pulled up outside Hull's Paragon Station Interchange. Gary gave the driver a wink and passed him a fifty pound note.

'Cheers, Gary.' The cabbie thought it was his birthday. Gary knew it was worth it. The bloke always kept his mouth shut. He watched as the cab did an illegal U-turn and headed off down Ferensway, disappearing into the traffic.

Gary Barnes mingled with the crowd of rail and bus travellers coming out of the interchange and crossing the main road, heading for the large department stores, and decided on a cup of coffee to help him get his thoughts together. He headed for Starbucks.

He didn't really know why his brother had been picked up, but he wasn't going to take any chances. He decided the only sensible option was to keep a low profile and stay out of the way for a couple of days to see what happened. Twenty minutes later, when the cappuccino was finished, he headed for the British Home Stores and bought himself a holdall and enough essentials to keep him clean and clothed during his absence. His next step was to book into the Humberview Motel on the northern edge of the city centre.

66

Nobody knew why it was called the Humberview. The motel was on one of the busiest junctions in the city, the only view being of streams of traffic along Freetown Way.

* * *

A bitterly cold wind was wind blowing off the docks as Marlowe and Gowan walked to their cars parked on the opposite side of the road. Marlowe, with Gowan hot on his heels, dashed across as soon as there was a gap in the traffic and headed back to Gordon Street. The Nokia tune burst into life in his pocket as he reached the car. He fished it out, hit the accept key and lifted it to his ear. 'Marlowe.'

'Colombo, its Trev. My lads have just picked up one of the Barnes brothers - Pete.'

'That's great, Trev. Thanks for letting me know. Put him in an interview room and let him sweat for a bit. Shouldn't be long now. We're on our way back. Have the coffee ready.'

'Piss off. What did your last slave die of?' Cleeves replied.

Marlowe hung up and smiled to himself at the response; it was just what he expected. He started the Mondeo and carefully manoeuvred out of the tightly spaced car park whereupon DI Gowan followed him back to the nick.

Sergeant Cleeves was in the reception area as they walked in. 'Bloody hell, that was quick. Are you two on speed? You can get arrested for that.' The Sergeant chuckled at his own joke. 'I've put him in number two.'

The DCI and the DI headed straight for Marlowe's office for a coffee and to decide on a plan of action before going to have a word with the Brother Grimm they were holding in custody. It didn't take them long to settle for the traditional good cop, bad cop routine.

* * *

Like the rest of the station, the interview rooms had been refurbished completely. As Marlowe opened the door to Room 2, the smell of emulsion and gloss paint invaded his nostrils. The vapours rising from the new carpet made him think of Shag Pile Charlie.

As they entered the room, the uniformed officer who had been sitting in the corner stood, gave them a nod and left the room.

The DCI gave Barnes his best smile and said, 'Pete! How are you doing? Long time, no see.'

Barnes stood and leant forward, resting his hands flat on the Formica-topped table. 'Look, Mr Marlowe, what's this about? If I'm under arrest, I want my brief.'

'Sit down, Pete. You're not under arrest, not yet, anyway,' Gowan assured him. 'We only want a little chat. You're free to go at any time.'

'If that's the case, I'm off,' Barnes declared, making a move to walk around the table towards the door.

'Sit down!' ordered the DI.

'You just said...' Barnes stammered. Reluctantly, he edged back to his chair and sat down.

'Come on, Pete. You know how it works. 'Vee' ask the questions,' said Marlowe, attempting a humorous Herr Flik voice, 'and if 'vee' like the answers, you can go.'

Nobody smiled, never mind laughed. Gowan inwardly cringed. Barnes folded his arms across his chest and rocked his chair back onto two legs, fixing his gaze on the DCI.

The two detectives sat on the tubular steel seats opposite Barnes. The room was quiet as Marlowe set down his manila folder and opened it, affecting to be studying the contents. Marlowe's belief was that a drawn-out stretch of silence gave villains time to ponder.

'Where's your brother?' asked the DI.

'How should I know? I'm his brother, not his bloody keeper,' Barnes replied tartly.

'Where were you on Sunday night?' Marlowe asked without looking up from the folder.

'At 'ome, watching telly,' said Barnes, picking at some dried skin on the side of his nose.

'On your own?' Gowan questioned.

'No, Gary was with me. We watched 'eartbeat on telly. Can't beat a bit of nostalgia, they 'ad decent coppers in them days.'

'All night? Sounds nice - a cosy night in front of the telly with a cup of tea.'

'No, when it finished, we got a taxi and went down the Sailor for a couple of pints.' Barnes examined the skin on his finger then flicked it on the floor.

'Did anybody see you?' Marlowe inquired.

'Course they bloody did. It's a pub, innit? We got there about 'alf nine and left at closing time.'

'Let's try something else, then.' Marlowe took a black and white photograph of the murdered man out of the folder and placed it in front of Barnes. 'Do you know this man?'

'Never seen 'im before in me life.' Pete Barnes moved his attention to his hands and started picking at dead skin around his bitten fingernails.

DI Gowan leaned across the table and matched Barnes's gaze, staring into his pockmarked face. 'It's funny, that.' The DI leaned closer. 'Can you tell me why he had your mobile number programmed into his phone?'

Barnes shifted in his seat and leant forward. ''Ere, let me 'ave another look. Oh yeah, think I do know 'im. Well not know 'im as such. We done a bit of business together. Saw 'is picture in the paper. Dead i'nt 'e?'

'What sort of business?' Marlowe cupped his hands together on the table in front of him. He knew Barnes was playing him.

'You know, a bit of this, a bit of that,' smirked Barnes.

'Come on, Pete. You can be a bit more specific than that, can't you? What about Sunday night? Did you do business with him then? What time did you leave the pub?'

'Like I said, closing time. Must have been getting on for 'alf eleven. Got a taxi.'

'You didn't stop off to meet Gleeson for a bit of business?'

'Piss off. I want my brief,' snarled Barnes through gritted teeth.

'He had some nasty bruising. I don't suppose you know anything about that either,' added the DI. 'Been on the Riverside Quay lately?'

'Oh, come on. Number one, I never saw 'im Sunday. We went straight home. Two, I 'aven't been on the Quay for years. Look, I've 'ad enough, Mr Marlowe. If you want me to answer any more questions, I want my solicitor 'ere. I'm not saying another bloody word.'

70

'No need for your brief, not yet. I think that will do us for now, Pete. You've been more than helpful,' said the DCI sarcastically.

'Don't go far now will you, Pete I'm sure we will want to have another friendly chat,' added DI Gowan.

As DCI Marlowe and DI Gowan left, the uniformed officer once more took up his place in the interview room. Gowan turned to the DCI. 'He thinks he's the dog's bollocks, that bloke.'

Marlowe smiled at the comment.

The DCI returned to his office while Dave Gowan headed for the custody area. He keyed in the door lock code and went into the office where Sergeant Cleeves was still working.

'Trevor, do me a favour will you? Keep Barnes for another hour or so before you let him out, just to piss him off.'

'No problem, Dave, I'll keep him all night, if you want!'

'If only we could,' Gowan muttered as he walked away.

* * *

DC Jonno Lawson and the TDC Lee Kristianson stood feeding coins into the vending machine out in the corridor as DCI Marlowe walked towards them. 'What's this then, lads? Another coffee break?'

'Just on the way back, Boss,' said Jonno as he turned to face the DCI.

'Where does this PI business come from, Jonno?' Lee asked quietly when Marlowe was out of earshot.

"What PI stuff?"

"I keep hearing it about. Marlowe, PI, gumshoe, you know...'

'Ah, that. Well, it's from before your time, son. In the sixties there used to be an American private investigator called Philip Marlowe, played by an actor called Robert Mitchum, hence the PI. Apparently this Marlowe's mam was obsessed with the character. There's loads of Marlowe films and books. You ought to give one a try. But be bloody careful. Whatever you do, don't call him it to his face. There's only Cleevsey who can get away with it. They've been mates since they were lads.'

The two collected their drinks and headed back to the squad room.

Chapter 7

The bed sheets were soaked in sweat and twisted in a knot around his feet. He tried to kick them off and free himself. Once he was untangled, he eased himself out of bed and sat on the edge. Reaching over, he switched on the bedside lamp and sat for a while with his head resting in his hands while the fuzziness cleared. Eventually he headed for the bathroom to wash away the sweat.

It was the same every night. Sweat and tears. Every night he was tortured by memories. That day was etched in his mind, clear and vivid - it would never leave him - the memory of walking through the front door into hell.

He'd been looking forward to coming home. He'd had a good day; his promotion at work had just come through and his long term career prospects were looking promising for the first time in years.

He arrived armed with a bottle of wine in one hand and a large bunch of flowers in the other. Time to celebrate, but the delight was not to last further than the front door where the stench hit him. His head reeled and his stomach turned in knots as the odour of vomit mixed with the coppery smell of blood reached his nostrils.

Slowly, as if in a dream, he closed the door behind him, walked through the carpeted hallway and hesitated, terrified at what he was going to find. He held his hand over his mouth, breathing between his fingers he caught his breath as he slowly moved to the lounge. His stomach heaved at what he saw.

It took all his self-control not to throw up. This was the first time he'd seen his son in six years, the first time since he'd thrown him out of the front door with his belongings in a black bin bag. He couldn't believe what he was seeing; it wasn't real, it couldn't be happening.

Fixed and staring as if in a trance, he was rooted to the spot. He did nothing to help his son as he lay on the living room floor, face down on the carpet in a pool his own vomit. A syringe lay on the floor beside him. He didn't know if his son was alive or dead. He didn't care. Raising his head, he looked beyond the living room to where his wife sat tied to a kitchen chair with her head tipped to the side. He rushed through the congealing lake of life's essential fluid and put his ear to his wife's mouth. Nothing. Then he felt for a pulse. Nothing. She was dead.

Afterwards, they put him on medication to give him some respite from the trauma of what he had just seen. It kicked in and, for a few hours, he too slept the sleep of the dead. But it couldn't eradicate the visions. Regardless of the medication he took from then on, all his nights remained haunted, some more than others. It was especially bad when he was hyped up; then the medication didn't work at all.

He remembered the last time when they had told him he could leave the hospital unit. "Don't worry, as long as you keep up with the medication, you should be fine. It's time to get your life back on track, get your life back."

'Frigging drugs,' he said aloud. 'What the hell do they know about what's happening inside my head? Bloody doctors, they know nowt about nowt.'

It had been two years, eleven months, two weeks and three days since he'd walked through that front door and he'd had three stays in the hospital since.

Was it vengeance he wanted? He just didn't know. All he knew was that it felt bloody good after the first one.

Me one – Them nil.

* * *

Detective Sergeant Jenny Bright lived right in the city centre; her apartment was in a brand new complex built above the Radio Humberside building, two minutes from Hull's Central Police Station. Her balcony offered a fantastic view of the city, right across to the River Humber. At night you could see the ships' lights twinkling as they travelled down the river.

She parked her Ford Focus in the underground parking area below the apartments, locked the vehicle and went up to the sixth floor via the lift.

As usual, the apartments were quiet. With the odd hours she worked, it was very rare for her to see her neighbours. Jenny unlocked the door and kicked off her shoes in the hallway. She glanced at herself in the full length mirror as she passed, and wasn't pleased at her reflection. She'd definitely looked better.

She opened the closet door and hung her coat inside, then went through to the kitchen diner. 'Food', she thought to herself, took a ready meal from the freezer and put it in the microwave - the police officer's staple diet, straight from

Marks and Spencer to the microwave. Taking an already-opened bottle of Chardonnay from the nearly empty fridge, she poured herself a generous glass and headed for the shower, taking her wine with her.

Feeling relaxed after her shower, she wrapped herself in her thick white towelling dressing gown and, with a towel tied around her wet hair, she headed back to the kitchen. The oven timer had long since pinged. She picked up the oven gloves off the unit, took out the container and emptied her dinner onto a plate. Next, she poured herself another glass of wine and went through to the lounge, carrying her dinner on a lap tray, and settled on the sofa facing the wall-mounted plasma television screen. With her meal balanced on her knee and her wine on the coffee table, she picked up the television's remote and channel hopped as she ate. It was funny, she thought. I bet most coppers eat this way, sat in front of the box.

There was the inevitable doom and gloom on the news channel, crappy reality shows or soaps she had no interest in. She settled for a soap.

When she'd finished eating, she put the empty plate on the coffee table in front of her, turned off the television and swapped the remote for the stereo controls, hitting the play button. With her glass of wine in her hand, she laid her head back on the sofa and started to unwind with Nora Jones.

The apartment intercom burst into life and startled her. 'Jenny, it's Dave.' Gowan called through the speaker.

Jenny rolled her eyes. So much for an easy night.

'Ok, come on up.' She moved into the hallway to stand by the door. Thirty seconds later, DI Dave Gowan stood in the doorway with a bottle of Shiraz in his hand.

'Well, this is a surprise. You'd better come in, seeing as you're bearing gifts.'

'Sorry for bursting in on you like this. Didn't know where else to go. I thought it was a better option than going out and getting legless.' Gowan knew Jenny's routine and kicked off his shoes in the hall before following her back into the living room where she resumed her position on the sofa and poured him a glass of wine. 'Come on, tell Aunty Jenny all about it.'

'Thanks. I appreciate this.' Gowan took off his jacket and laid it neatly on the floor before settling his lanky frame into the Ronnie Corbett sized easy chair.

'Don't tell me, it's Joan,' Jenny guessed correctly.

'How did you know? Am I that transparent?' Gowan reached across for his wine.

'I've known you long enough,' Jenny picked up the stereo controls and turned the volume lower. 'It's usually when you've had a row with Joan that I get a visit.'

'It's not really Joan's fault. I went round to her mother's to see the kids and try to sort some things out, but the interfering old bag just wouldn't leave us alone. Every time the conversation started to get friendly, she had to stick her oar in and wind us both up.'

'And...' Jenny pushed herself into the corner of the sofa, tucked her feet beneath her and took a sip of her wine.

'And, as usual, it ended in a blazing row. Funny thing is when the Wicked Witch of the West isn't around, we get on quite well. Anyway, as you'd expect, I lost it, used a few ill-chosen words, stormed out slamming the door behind me, and here I am.'

'At least I'm coming in handy for something,' said Jenny sarcastically.

'Sorry, didn't mean to make it sound like that. I walked around a bit and just needed a friendly face, bought a bottle of vino and here I am, turning up like the bad penny.'

Dave stretched out his legs and stood up, then went into the kitchen and came back with the corkscrew. He sat down again, opened the bottle of Shiraz and refilled their glasses. The conversation was easy and relaxed, and the time passed quickly. Eventually the conversation came around to work, as it usually did when they met socially.

'Not having much luck, are we?' Gowan commented.

'Slow start, but we usually get there in the end,' said Jenny as she leaned forward to pick up the controls and change the music.

'It's this nail business that gets me. Seems a bit ritualistic for our neck of the woods. I mean, this doesn't happen in Hull.'

'Yeah, I've had similar thoughts.' Jenny made herself more comfortable among the sofa cushions. 'It's obviously some nutter. Just hope it doesn't escalate into anything further. Pour me another glass of vino, will you?'

'Did I tell you what young Lee said? He thinks the bloke we are after is straight out of Sean Bean, some kind of eighteenth century torturer from Sharpe.'

By eleven o'clock, the second wine bottle was empty. 'I'm knackered, Dave. What are you doing - staying or going?' asked Jenny as she yawned.

'You know what? I feel too settled to go out there in the cold; you know, good company, nice wine and all that.' Gowan had a pleading smile on his face.

'I thought as much.' Jenny stood up from the sofa and headed off to the bathroom. 'You know where the spare room is. I'll get you a toothbrush. Good night.'

Chapter 8

The weather had turned distinctly colder overnight. The super-structure of the Daisy glistened in a covering of frost. Snow was forecast for later in the week.

Marlowe got on the road before the early rush started. The drive through to Hull from Beverley was for once an easy journey and Marlowe was in his office by seven o'clock. Indeed, he was so early he missed Cleavsey and his un-witty PI jokes, and by the time the team started to arrive in the squad room, he was on his second cup of coffee and had managed to get through quite a bit of the paperwork that had mounted up over the last couple of days.

He knocked on his office window and signalled to Kristianson as he saw the young TDC enter the squad office. Lee did an about-turn, knocked on Marlowe's door and went in.

'Sit down.' Marlowe instructed. 'How are things going with the off-licence break-ins?'

Lee sat opposite the DCI, feeling slightly apprehensive. 'Fine, Boss. All sorted.'

Marlowe was amazed. 'Ok, fill me in on the details.' He pushed his chair away from the desk and sat back to listen to the particulars.

'Uniform responded to both of last night's two break-ins, No finesse, just brute force to gain access, namely a crowbar. Luckily, Boozy Buys on Newland Avenue had CCTV that actually worked. Two uniforms were still on the scene talking with the manager when I got down there.'

'You didn't step back and let them run things?' Marlowe said with an edge to his voice.

'No way. Anyway, we watched the footage in the manager's office and one of the uniform lads, Wayne, recognised one of the faces. Gordon Anderson. Lives down Hawthorn Avenue. He's been pulled quite a few times for all manner of petty stuff. We went straight round and, believe it or not, the van, still full of booze and fags, was parked up outside. The front door to the house was even unlocked so we went in and there they were. Both of them had been sampling the stuff they'd nicked. Pissed as newts, they were, and half asleep, sprawled out on the sofa. We brought them back and put them in the cells while they sobered up, then charged them.'

'Are they still enjoying our hospitality?' asked the DCI.

'No. Once they'd sobered up, Sergeant Cleeves bailed them for seven days pending a date for the court appearance, and let them go.'

'Ok, good job, Lee. Let me have the paperwork when it's sorted.'

Lee stood up and nodded to the DCI, feeling pleased with himself. It had been his first solo job. He returned to the squad room with a grin on his face stretching from ear to ear.

Marlowe followed him out into the main office. 'Morning all. Thought I'd come in early to keep an eye on you lot.'

'Ha, ha, yeah, yeah.'

Marlowe, with coffee in hand, stood in front of the whiteboard. He noticed that more crime scene pictures had been added - larger, better copies, monochrome this time, stark and real alongside the colour prints.

'Right, you lot, here we go again. What have we got?' He looked over to DS Bright. 'Jenny?'

'His car was clean, Boss. Forensic did a thorough job, didn't come up with anything: no prints but his own. His car was as clean as his house. Uniform are still going through the city centre CCTV system trying to track its movements from the Asda at Kingswood to Hessle Road where the car was found.'

DC Jonno Lawson was next. He stood to face the rest of the team and read from his notes. 'It's as we thought. He was relatively new to Hull but he didn't mess about. He pretty quickly established a good customer base with the student community in the Beverley Road and been thrown out and warned off about his dealing in most of the Beverley Road pubs. On a weekend he concentrated on the bars and clubs nearer the town centre.'

'Get anything from his computer?' the DCI asked Tanya.

'Only the usual stuff. He did his banking online with Barclays. Had a small overdraft of one hundred and fifty pounds and both his credit cards were all paid up to date. A number of porn sites were stored in his favourites: no surprise there. If he was making plenty of money, he wasn't

82

keeping it in a bank. I'll dig a bit further, try and find if there is any money in any other accounts anywhere.'

Marlowe pulled up a chair and sat, nodding to Gowan to take over.

'Me and the Boss did our bit yesterday. We spoke to the landlord of the Criterion and he recognised the victim.'

'Was he a regular?' asked Tanya.

'No, the landlord saw him leave before closing time with another bloke who could be our suspect.'

'Have we a description?' This time the question came from Jonno.

'Yes, I'll let you have a copy at the end of the briefing. I also met someone on the Quay who thinks our man might have been a carpenter according to the sign writing on the van. The description of the van he gave might link in with the CCTV pictures.'

'Same bloke who was in the Criterion?' DS Bright asked as she looked up from her notes.

'Could well be. He gave a similar description.'

'Anyone?' Marlowe threw the question open and waited. 'Anything else to add?' No response. Marlowe took the floor once more. 'Ok at least it looks like we might be getting somewhere. Take over please, Dave.'

Marlowe went back into his glass cubicle and stood by the window, warming his hands on the radiator. Ten minutes later, DI Gowan knocked on the door and came through juggling two cups of coffee, setting them down on the desk.

'Cheers, Dave. Have a seat.' Marlowe moved away from the window, sat behind his desk and picked up his coffee.

'If this bloke couldn't afford the rent on the Quay, there's a chance he might have found another workshop.'

'I've already got it covered; Lee's checking with the business letting agencies. It might take a while; there's more than we thought. The bugger thinks he's top of the class since the off-licence thing got sorted.'

They both smiled.

'Could get Jonno to check around to see if anyone's sighted anybody resembling the suspect,' the DCI suggested. 'You never know what he might throw up. He's got some very funny contacts. Did Tanya find out anything more about Gleeson's financial situation?'

'No, she's still trawling through it. She's contacted financial services to check all the banks and building societies, but it's not looking good so far.'

'Have uniform had any sightings of the van?'

'The description's been circulated, but with so little to go on nothing positive's come up.'

'Ok, Dave, keep me informed.' Marlowe pushed back his chair, stretched out his arms above his head and sighed, then brought his attention back to the computer screen.

* * *

For the past fifty minutes, TDC Kristianson had been sitting at his desk with the telephone handset glued to his ear when the DI came back into the squad room.

'Thank you very much, Miss. You've been very helpful. I'll see you shortly.' Lee was feeling elated as he put the receiver down. 'Might have something, sir,' he said to the DI. 'That was a receptionist from a letting agency down Springbank Avenue. From the description I gave her, she thinks she might have seen our man. I'll get down there now.'

'What did she sound like?' Gowan asked.

'Quite nice, actually.'

'Well don't forget why you're there!' ribbed Gowan as the TDCs face coloured up.

Marlowe was frustrated with the way the case was going and his eyes ached from staring at his computer monitor. He took off his spectacles and rubbed his fingertips into his temples. Time for a cigarette break, he thought, putting his spectacles back on and heading for the station car park.

Sergeant Cleeves had beaten him to it and was already standing in the cold with his hands deep in his pockets and a roll-up hanging from his lips.

'How's it going, Trev?' asked the DCI.

'Not too bad, Phil, it's a bit quiet at the minute. Are you having any luck with the Quay murder?'

'If I'm being honest, no. We need a break and quick.' Marlowe pulled up his jacket collar around his neck, took his cigarettes out of his pocket and pulled out a Benson's. 'I've already got the Super on my back. If things don't start to happen soon, Central will be all over the case like a rash.' The DCI flipped open his lighter, lit the cigarette and blew smoke into the air. He was ready for his nicotine fix.

'How's life on the ocean waves? I bet its bloody cold this weather!' Trev smiled, referring to Marlowe's narrow boat home.

'No, not really. Get the heat on and have a nice bottle of plonk, you'd be surprised.' The DCI shivered. 'Can't stop out here, though, Trev. It's too bloody cold.' Marlowe took another deep drag on the cigarette, stubbed it out in the ash bucket and went back inside, leaving the sergeant alone in the car park.

* * *

Lee was lucky. He was able to pull the pool car to the kerb edge right outside the Alliance Business Letting Agency. Before getting out, he spent a moment checking his hair in the rear view mirror.

The premises were a double fronted building on a busy parade of shops wedged between a charity shop and a home bakery.

'Good morning, sir. Can I help you?' The pretty, young receptionist asked.

Lee was more than impressed meeting the young lady face-to-face. She looked even better than she sounded on the telephone, so he gave her his best smile.

'I'm TDC Lee Kristianson, from Gordon Street Police Station. Are you the young lady I spoke with on the telephone about half an hour ago, Mandy, isn't it?'

'Yes, that's me. It's about the murder, isn't it?' she asked excitedly.

Without waiting to be asked, Lee sat in the chrome chair facing the receptionist. 'Sort of. You told me on the phone you might have seen someone resembling the description I gave you.'

'Well, I can't be certain. We get a lot of self-employed people in here looking for premises. Coffee?' She beamed a great big smile at him.

'That would be great, thanks.' Lee studied the photographs on the office wall while she went off to the coffee machine. Still smiling, Mandy brought back the drinks and put Lee's coffee down in front of him.

He couldn't help watching her as she walked back around the desk. 'Thanks. Right, Mandy, what can you tell me?' He took out his notebook.

Mandy sat back in her chair and crossed her legs. The TDC's gaze followed her movements as she did so.

'I think it was one afternoon around two weeks ago. We usually get the smartly dressed Hi Tech type coming in here for premises, that's why I remember. We don't get many workman types like this chap.'

'Can you describe him?'

'Tallish, about five feet ten, I would think. He had quite long brown hair, combed straight back, and a thin face - a worried type of face.'

'Remember anything else? Eyes, nose?' Lee looked up from taking notes.

'Well, not really, only the way he was dressed. I remember because he wore a black coat a bit like the type my dad wears for work, woollen, I think, three quarter length with buttons down both sides of the front, and patch pockets. Dark coloured trousers - could have been navy blue, but not jeans - and he was wearing black shoes,' Mandy said as she shifted in her seat and crossed her legs the other way, causing Lee's eyes to get sidetracked again.

'Apart from the description, what makes you think it's the man we want to talk to?'

'He told me he was thinking of going into the building trade. That's what made me give you a call; you mentioned something like that on the phone. Oh, and he said he wanted somewhere cheap.'

'Did you show him any premises?'

'No, while we were talking, Mr Maxwell, the Manager came in and took over. I think he may have shown him one or two.'

'Do you have a name and address for him?'

'No, I haven't. Mr Maxwell might.'

'Is Mr Maxwell in, Mandy?' asked the TDC.

'No, he's in Ireland on holiday for a few days.'

'When's he due back?'

'He comes back at the weekend, but not back to work until Monday.'

Mandy picked up her coffee, blew on it daintily and sipped.

Lee jotted the dates down in his notebook. 'That's great Mandy. You have been really helpful.'

Mandy leaned forward, put her elbows on the desk and rested her head in her hands, smiling at the young TDC. 'Anytime. More than happy to help.' She gave him a broad smile as he stood ready to leave.

'I'll leave you my card.' Lee fumbled in his wallet. 'I would appreciate a call as soon as Mr Maxwell gets back.' Lee stretched out his arm to shake hands, holding Mandy's hand a fraction longer than he should have done. He could feel the colour rising in his cheeks. 'Bye then. I'll be in touch.'

Mandy waved his card in the air as he left.

Chapter 9

The mobile vibrated, then rang in his pocket. 'Where the bloody hell are you?' Pete Barnes yelled into the receiver as he reached across the sofa arm and put his can of Smooth on the floor.

'Humberview Motel. When I saw you get picked up, I decided I'd better make myself scarce for a while. What were they after?'

'Asking about Gleeson - cheeky sods thought we had done him in.'

'You didn't tell them anything?'

'What do you take me for? I can handle them,' Pete said sharply. This was something Gary doubted very much. Pete had more bravado than brains.

'Ok, I guess it's time to come back. I'll see you later.' Gary Barnes settled himself back on the unmade motel bed with a bottle from the mini bar. The decision had already been made before the telephone conversation. He'd already decided to leave the motel, and his bag was packed and ready for the off.

He picked up the room telephone and ordered a taxi back to the Copse Mead. Gary always worried when he left his brother to his own devices. He'd warned him time and time again, but Pete still took no notice and insisted on doing a deal or two.

* * *

Apart from the pub users milling about, St. Stephen's Square was relatively quiet. It was only two minutes' walk from the city centre at the back of the new transport interchange. The face of the city was changing drastically, sometimes for the better, sometimes for the worse.

A few dim orange glowing streetlights illuminated the area as the Ford Transit turned the corner. The driver noticed one of the overhead headlights wasn't working at the far end of the square, away from the red brick Providence public house. He quickly scanned the area and slowed the vehicle down, pulling into the kerbside nearly under the unlit lamp. This position offered a good view of the alley beside the pub. Turning off the lights and killing the engine, he settled back in the driving seat, pulled his coat tight around him, and pushed his hands into his pockets and watched.

At 10.30 p.m., he saw him. He'd been watching him for three weeks. He'd been watching them all, the dregs of society who dealt in the misery of others. Some he knew by name, some he didn't. He knew their routes and their routines - which pub, which night and what time.

The scruffy looking man came out of the pub and checked the scene from left to right. He took out a tobacco tin from the pocket of his denim jacket and rolled a cigarette, lighting it with a Zippo lighter. He looked in all directions around the square, then, with the roll-up hanging from his lips, he put his hands in his pockets.

Unconsciously he flicked back his lank hair and hunched up his shoulders against the cold, taking a deep drag from the roll-up as he walked towards the alley by the side of the pub. Out of the sight of prying eyes, he stood and waited.

He didn't have to wait very long. Two minutes later, he was followed out by a young girl. Despite the freezing cold, she was only wearing a skimpy top and jeans. She hadn't bothered with a jacket. The driver of the Ford Transit reckoned she looked barely more than eighteen.He watched the transaction take place. The girl handed over cash in exchange for a small packet and slipped it into her bag before returning to the pub. Others followed suit and this process went on for the next twenty minutes or so, cash changing hands for little plastic packets. Six customers in twenty-five minutes - *Must be making some tidy money*, the driver thought as he watched and waited. When no more punters came out of the pub, the man in the denim jacket went back inside.

The driver decided the time was right. He climbed down from the driver's seat and locked the van. It was getting colder and the clear night had produced a frost, which glistened on the nineteenth century cobbles, making them like glass. He walked across the cobbled square towards the Providence and stood beneath the same brass light, composing himself. 'Not long now,' he mumbled as he went into the pub. It was less than an hour to closing time. He pushed his way through the crowd milling around the bar and ordered a pint of mild. With the pint in his hand, he stood watching his quarry, waiting for the right moment.

If anybody had been watching forty five minutes later, they would not have thought much about it, just two mates coming out of a pub, one sober and one pissed. The driver liked to use Rohypnol. The good thing about this date-rape drug was that the effects weren't so pronounced. The victim might not be aware of what was happening to them, but they could still move their limbs. He simply had to help him to the van and put him in the passenger seat, fasten the seat belt and drive off.

Easy. It had been easy.

'Now you just sit there and behave yourself,' he advised his unresponsive victim in the passenger seat. 'Won't be long now, then we'll see how hard you are.'

Denim Jacket never said a word. He couldn't - he was numb with the drug, just sitting there, lolling in the seat, listless.

The lock-up was only a ten minute drive away at that time of night - into Park Street, over the bridge, a right onto Anlaby Road and five minutes beyond that.

There was no sign of life as he turned down Havelock Street. When he reached the cul-de-sac, he turned off the van lights and watched the velvet pelts of the rats scurrying as they heard the engine noise. His adrenaline was pumping. It felt like his heart was beating a hole in his chest.

He pulled the van up right outside the lock-up's doors and left Denim Jacket Man sitting there while he opened .He took the key from the chain hanging on his belt, put it in the sturdy lock, removed the padlock and went inside.

The first thing he did was to check the sacking over the window was still covering the grimy glass. He didn't turn on the light until he had Denim Jacket Man inside.

Everything was ready. The plastic sheeting was on the floor and the chair was set in the centre. There was no struggle; he just led his victim in and sat him on the wooden chair.

Denim Jacket offered no resistance whatsoever as he slumped down on the wooden chair while his kidnapper quickly and quietly donned his protective suit and gloves. He picked up a roll of parcel tape off the workbench and wrapped it tight around Denim Jacket's body and arms, securing him to the chair back. Next, he secured each ankle to a chair leg. Denim Jacket was fixed, unable to move. He was at one with the chair, head hanging down onto his chest, still unaware of the danger he was in. He didn't even flinch when his kidnapper grabbed him roughly by the hair and yanked back his head.

The kidnapper stared into the man's dead eyes as he sealed his victim's mouth tightly closed with the parcel tape. As the adrenaline pumped through his body, he could feel the sweat trickle down his back inside his overalls. His hands trembled as he fumbled with the plastic lighter, trying to light the candle stuck onto the workbench. Next, he mixed his cocktail of drugs and carefully heated them up in the bowl of the spoon his son had used. *Ironic,* he thought to himself. He held the spoon over the flickering flame until the contents bubbled. He then picked up the hypodermic syringe off the bench and sucked the deadly infusion through the needle.

93

Denim Jacket was still oblivious to what was going on as the needle pricked the back of his hand and the plunger released its deadly cocktail into his body. His eyes rolled into his head and closed. His head dropped forward, his chin resting on his chest. The sweat dripped down the kidnapper's forehead. He wiped it clear with the back of a gloved hand and moved on to the next stage. Timing was critical, as it had to be done before the drugs finished him.

He walked back to the workbench and took a four inch nail from the side pocket of the tool bag. With the nail in his gloved hand and his twenty ounce claw hammer in the other, he stood directly in front of his victim. With the hand holding the nail, he pushed the head into the upright position and held it steady with his left hand. He placed the nail precisely on the crown of the head and took a deep breath, bringing the hammer arcing up in the air. Then, on the out breath, *whack*, once.

The victim's eyes opened wide in shock, but the drugs suppressed the pain. The driver's hand gripped the hammer shaft tighter this time, his arm stretched high above him, then down, *whack*, for the final time. The nail head flattened into the skull.

The drug had already taken the victim to another place and the only sound he made was a slight moaning when he bit into his tongue as his head jolted down into his neck. Blood ran down his forehead, trickling along the sides of the parcel tape and along his chin.

Although this wasn't his first time, the killer just made it to the dirty enamel sink basin in time to throw up. His stomach heaved as he retched for a full five minutes. 'Job done,' he called aloud. 'Me two, them nil.'

He turned out the workshop light, made his way to the window and moved aside the piece of sacking that covered the grimy glass. He peered out through the dirt. He could see nothing but darkness. Even the rats had gone.

He let the sacking fall back into place over the window and switched the light back on, turning his attention to the figure laid out on the floor. He could still taste the bile in his throat.

The thick plastic sheeting was difficult to handle through the workman's gloves he was wearing. Kneeling down, he pulled it tight around the body, wrapping the still figure like a carpet and binding him around the feet and middle. He then pulled the plastic firmly around the head and taped it too. Once more he returned to the window checking outside before he made his next move.

There was still nobody in sight, just darkness.

He stared down at the plastic wrapped figure on the floor and once again killed the light. He slid the bolt on the door, opened it and went into the darkness. His van was as close to the door as he could get it. He opened its side door and returned to the centre of the workshop. Sweat was still dripping down his face as he bent down and grabbed the plastic.

It wasn't heavy. The man didn't weigh much, but the gloves hampered his grip, making it difficult to handle. Half dragging and half lifting, he managed to manoeuvre his package from the workshop, leaving a trail on the oily floor.

He heaved the bundle into the van, slid the van door closed as quietly as he could, and turned back to the workshop. Just as quietly, he snapped the padlock shut and secured the door.

'Right,' he said to himself, 'time to move.'

He walked around the van to the driver's side, opened the door and climbed in. He sighed as he settled into the driving seat, feeling his body relax after the exertion. The mist in his eyes was clearing; things were clearer in his head now too.

Still wearing his coveralls and gloves, he put the key in the ignition and turned it. 'Bet he could do with a couple of aspirins.'

He laughed aloud. He could feel the pressure easing. With the lights turned off, he manoeuvred the van out of the cul-de-sac.

Chapter 10

On board the Daisy, Marlowe was also feeling relaxed. It had gone ten o'clock by the time he'd driven back to Beverley and he had decided on a quick Marks and Spencer pasta meal from the freezer for his late dinner. Once it was ready, he took it through into the saloon. More than the food, he enjoyed savouring the Morella cherry taste of the glass of dark ruby French Rasteau Reserve. He finished his pasta and carried his dishes into the galley to clear away later.

Marlowe picked up the half-full bottle of wine and poured himself another large glass. He took his coat off the rack near the solid fuel boiler and put it on, then picked up his packet of Bensons.

On the nights he didn't fall asleep in the dinette, he would go on the Daisy's after-deck for a smoke before bed while Archie had a wonder about on the towpath. He picked up the glass and, with the dog by his side, he opened the hatch. The cold hit him as soon as the wooden door was opened. He put down the glass on the top of the cabin and fumbled in his pocket for his cigarettes. He took out a Benson's and placed it in his mouth. With both hands he cupped the lighter against the biting wind and lit the cigarette.

On summer nights, Marlowe would sit here for hours drinking and smoking, just listening to the water rippling against the sides of the boat as Archie rummaged in the long grass. The weather had really changed over the past couple of days from wet and miserable to cold bright days. Marlowe could see the stars as he sipped the wine and looked towards the clear night sky. A keen frost had already taken hold, covering the superstructure of the narrow boat. The Beck looked almost mystical as it shimmered in the frosty moonlight.

He stood savouring his surroundings. His peace was soon disturbed. Down below in the galley his mobile was trilling out the Nokia tune. *Bloody hell*, he thought. He stubbed out the cigarette and, with his wine in his hand, he went below, closing the hatch behind him as the dog scampered past. 'Marlowe,' he barked into the mobile.

'Boss, there's been another one.' It was DI Gowan.

'Jesus, what the bloody hell's going on?' Marlowe put down the wine glass on the worktop. 'Where?'

'Wiltshire Road, service road underneath the Hessle Road flyover. Got the call from the station a couple of minutes ago.'

'You'd better get them to send a car for me. I'm probably over the limit,' the DCI said, massaging his temples with his fingers.

'Will do, I'll meet you at the scene.'

Marlowe shut down the mobile, filled the kettle and switched it on. 'Better have a quick coffee and sober up a bit before the car gets here,' he said to his canine friend. Harry from the lock keeper's cottage would come and get Archie when morning arrived.

The DCI was still sorting himself out when he heard a siren approaching. 'That's all we need, "blues and twos". It'll wake the neighbours and the bloody ducks, won't it, boy?'

* * *

The flyover was at the western end of Hessle Road where it changed names to Hessle High Road adjoining the Wiltshire Road Industrial Estate. The killer had picked another secluded place, especially in the night time hours, thought Marlowe.

The area was desolate, with no direct access to the industrial estate as it was a side service road for rail maintenance.

As the squad car pulled up, Marlowe could see the scene was a hive of activity close to the railway tracks.

'Thanks for the lift,' he said to the PC who had collected him. Getting out of the car, he stood and surveyed the murder scene. It was already cordoned off, with the standard blue and white plastic incident tape, fixed to lampposts some 100 metres from the main action. The floodlights had already been set up, illuminating the main area.

Marlowe had wrapped himself in his City scarf and woolly hat before he left the vehicle. He stood by the car, took a pair of latex gloves from his jacket pocket and put them on.

Dave Gowan was the first to see him arrive and walked towards him. 'Bloody hell, Dave, I'm getting too old to be coming out at this time of night,' grumbled Marlowe as he hunched his shoulders against the frosty night. 'It's a hell of a place. How come we found out so soon? Was the area car skiving off?'

'No. Would you believe me if I told you a tramp phoned it in on his mobile?'

'Now you are taking the piss. Who called it in?'

'Seriously, like I said, it was a tramp. Said he carried the phone for emergencies. First time he's used it since he got the bloody thing.' Dave was still unsure if the DCI believed him.

'Let's go and have a look, then, before we have a word with this homeless person. Get that, Dave? We don't use the word 'tramp' anymore. Remember, you've done the courses.'

'What the hell do you think you are doing?' a woman's voice called out as Marlowe passed under the plastic tape. 'You can't come in here. Can't you see this is a crime scene?'

'And you are?' asked Marlowe.

'I'm Karina Taylor, the Chief Scene of Crime Officer.'

'Nice to meet you, Karina, I'm the Boss.' Marlowe held up his warrant card for her to see in the glare of the floodlights.

'Oh, sorry, sir. Just following procedures.' Karina pulled down the hood of her white coveralls, letting her long fair hair fall loose around her oval face.

'Where's Brice?'

'He's had an accident, sir; I thought you would have been informed.'

'What sort of accident?' Marlowe asked as he watched the SOCO team in their protective clothing searching the area. His eyes wandered. He could see the photographer hunched down over a bundle of plastic and another SOCO roaming around with a video camera.

'Fell off his bike on the way in. Said he skidded on the ice. He's sat waiting in Casualty now. Looks like he broke his leg.'

'Silly old sod, I told him he should get the station to send a car for him.' Marlowe couldn't help but laugh out loud. 'OK, Karina, I won't spoil your crime scene. Tell me what we've got and drop the 'sir'.'

'Right, sir. Sorry, I mean 'right'.'

Dave Gowan had already assigned a team of uniformed officers to search the far perimeter of the crime scene, whilst the SOCO specialists worked within the immediate area. Karina led Marlowe to where the victim lay close to the rail track amongst the dead brambles and long dead grass.

'He's picked another good spot out of sight from anyone accessing the service road under the flyover. Obviously he didn't bank on our friend finding him so soon,' Marlowe observed. Karina nodded her head in acknowledgement as she pulled back on her hood, tucking her blonde hair into it.

Marlowe could see the body was covered in plastic sheeting and fastened tight with parcel tape, as the previous victim had been. With the body still wrapped tight, there was very little for Marlowe to examine. Going with his

101

better instinct, except for a quick look, he held back and didn't touch anything.

Karina bent down and crouched by the victim. With a pen she eased the plastic away from the victim's face. The eyes were wide open. Karina had a thing about eyes. She'd had it since she was a child and she shuddered as the victim's dead eyes stared back at her. She hated eyes - alive or dead. She felt physically sick.

Marlowe noticed the trickle of blood from the crown of the head also seeping from the tape over the mouth. 'If you look over here,' Karina pointed to a spot a couple of metres away, 'you can see tyre tracks in the frost, and can you see the scuff marks?'

'Looks like he pulled the body from the vehicle and dragged it to where it is now.' The DCI surveyed the vicinity, trying to visualise what might have happened. 'Get some pictures of the tyre tracks while we still have the frost. We might be able to get a make on the vehicle. OK, Karina, I'll leave you to it. Soon as you have anything, let me know right away.'

'Will do, sir.'

'Dave, where's the bloke that rang it in?' Marlowe was flapping his arms around his body to keep the circulation going as he walked across to where the DI stood writing in his notebook.

'Over there.' The DI pointed to a squad car just beyond the perimeter tape. 'Follow your nose, you can't miss him. His name's Gazzer,' he added as they both walked over to the squad car.

'Fancy a coffee to warm you up, sir?' asked one of the uniformed officers who'd had the foresight to bring along a couple of thermos flasks. 'Just what I need. Thanks,' the DCI said as he accepted a steaming polystyrene cup. Gowan shot the constable a glance that could have killed.

'One for you, sir?' asked the constable as an afterthought when he read the look on the DI's face. Gowan nodded.

Both men carried their steaming cups over to the patrol car where the homeless person sat with an officer. Even though it was freezing, Marlowe noticed the vehicle's windows were wide open and the PC had his head hanging out, trying not to breathe too deeply.

The DCI had a brilliant idea. 'I'll tell you what, Dave. You go and have a quick word with the witness while I have a look around.' Marlowe couldn't help but smile as he spoke. 'Then get one of the lads to take him to the nick.'

'But - but I thought you'd want to speak to him first hand, you know, get the information straight from the horse's mouth, so to speak,' the DI protested in vain.

'No, that's alright, Dave, I have every confidence. I can interview him back at the station.'

With his back to the DI, Marlowe still had a smile on his face. Away in the shadows, he could see a form of structure made up of cardboard boxes and wooden pallets erected in between two concrete pillars.

'Our friends accommodation,' he mumbled to himself. Just as well it was out of the way, he thought, or the witness might have become a victim too.

He decided to put off taking a closer look until daylight. Leaving Jenny Bright and Tanya at the scene, Marlowe and

Gowan made their way through the frosty night to the Gordon Street station. An unfortunate PC had the task of driving the witness back to the nick with the vehicle's windows wide open to the freezing night.

* * *

With the odour flowing from the witness like a pungent cloud, the DCI decided to listen to what Gazzer had to say in one of the interview rooms rather than in his office. Marlowe, Gowan and the witness sat informally around the Formica table with cups of coffee in front of them. The man who sat opposite had tight curly hair that could have done with a wash on top of a grimy red alcohol-veined face. He was wearing an army great coat tied at the waist with a leather belt, dirty combat trousers and scuffed boots.

'Ok Gazzer, before we start, can you tell us your full name?' opened Gowan.

'Turner, Gary Turner.' The dishevelled witness shifted uneasily in his seat, not sure if he was in trouble or not.

'My name's DCI Marlowe, and this chap whom you've already met at the scene is DI Dave Gowan. There's no need to worry, you're not in any bother. Just tell us in your own words exactly what you saw.'

'Well, I'd got the tarpaulin pulled over the opening of me boxes, I was just getting into me sleeping bag, then I 'eard it.'

'Heard what?' asked the DCI.

'An engine, loud like a diesel motor. Anyway, I turned off me calor gas lamp and moved the tarp a bit to look out, like. It was a dark coloured Transit, one of them newish small types. It'd pulled up just near the bushes next to the tracks, like. Anyway, me being a bit nosey like, I kept watching. Have to, you see. You don't know if its kids coming to try and sort you out. It's happened before.'

'What happened next?' Gowan asked, picking up his mug of coffee and holding it in both hands as if warming them.

'I saw 'im dump it. The driver turned off the lights, got out of the cab, 'ad a quick look around, then 'e went around to the side, like, I could see 'im sliding open the door.'

'Saw him dump what?' asked Marlowe.

'I couldn't tell at first. It looked like a bundle of carpet. I thought it was just rubbish. 'E pulled it out the van and dragged it to the edge near the rail tracks. Anyway, as soon as I was sure 'e'd gone, I went across to have a look, like. That's when I realized what it was.'

'Then what?' asked Dave, chewing the end of his pen.

'Went back in me shelter for me mobile. It was a good job it had a full battery. I don't often get a chance to charge it up, like, and then called you lot. Don't suppose there's any chance of a fag?'

'Soon. Did you know the man?'

'Nah, but there was a name on the side of the van.' Marlowe leaned closer across the table, holding his breath, partly in anticipation and partly in reaction to the smell, hoping this could be the break he had been waiting for. "Ian Ball', it said. On the side, like. Carpenter. The letters looked as if someone had tried to scrape 'em off, but I could just make it out.'

'Could you see any telephone numbers on the van?' asked the DCI.

'There might have been but I didn't take much notice.'

'Can you describe him?' Marlowe asked, lifting his eyes from his notes.

'As I said, it was pretty dark. 'E looked to be about five-ten tall, maybe six feet. I'm sure 'e was wearing dark overalls, 'e 'ad the 'ood down but I couldn't see 'im properly. Thin face and 'is 'air was combed straight back, about collar length.'

'You've been very helpful, Gazzer,' Marlowe told him. 'Look, you can't go back to your shelter tonight, not with all that's going on down there. Fancy a night in a warm cell?'

'Not under arrest am I?'

'No, it'll be better than walking the street on a night like this. We'll leave the door open.'

'Brill!' Gazzer's face lit up at the prospect of spending the night in the warmth, even if it was in a police cell.

'Sorry, but the custody sergeant will have my arse if we give you bed and breakfast without you getting cleaned up a bit first. If you remember anything else, let one of my colleagues know.'

Marlowe turned to the constable sat in the corner. 'Can you sort that out? Let Gary get cleaned up, sort him some clothes from lost property and find him something hot to eat.'

'Thanks, Mr. Marlowe. Can I 'ave that fag now?'

'Just one more question, Gazzer. How come you have a mobile phone? I'm just curious, that's all.'

'I do some odd jobs around the industrial estate and the bloke down at the removal company gave it me, you know, so 'e could get 'old of me when 'e has a job, like.'

'Cheers, Gazzer. You can have that fag now.'

* * *

'What's Gazzer's story, Dave, any idea?' the DCI asked as they made their way back to the squad room.

'Six years with the Yorkshire Regiment. He's done the lot - three tours of Northern Island, the first Gulf War and two tours in Bosnia.' They watched the constable lead Gazzer out of the office. 'It's the usual story. He left the regiment when his time was up and just couldn't cope with everyday life. Nightmares, mood swings. The thing that finished it off was when he started to get stroppy, and frightened the family. Sad, when you think about it.'

Marlowe shook his head. 'I hate to think what the poor sod's seen. There's no wonder the bugger has cracked up.'

Chapter 11

It had been a long night, with Marlowe cat napping on the office settee. He stood staring out of his office window into the frost covered car park, mulling over the previous night's events. Another hour or so and it would be light.

After two weeks of frustration with no significant leads, Marlowe was at last starting to feel positive. With the information gleaned from Gary Turner - the homeless person - they now had a positive link to the vehicle spotted on the CCTV, and a possible name for the suspect.

Marlowe crossed his office to the coffee machine, poured himself a cup and sat behind his desk. DS Bright passed his window. The DCI caught her attention and beckoned her to come in.

Jenny knocked on the door once and entered,

'Take a seat, Jenny,' Marlowe said, waving her towards the sofa. 'Any news from SOCO?'

The DCI wasn't the only one feeling the worse for wear. Jenny Bright didn't look too bright after a night without sleep either.

'Karina confirmed what we already guessed - same as the first victim, bloody great nail in the head. She's checking the plastic and tape for fingerprints and DNA as we speak.'

'What time's the post-mortem?'

'They're trying to fit it in late morning,' Jenny replied, trying to stifle a yawn behind the back of her hand.

'Have we got an ID on him yet?'

Jenny plonked a plastic evidence bag containing the victim's belongings down on the desk. 'We've been fortunate with this one - mobile, debit card and driving licence. On top of that he was already known to us. His name's James Wood, twenty two. He lived down North Road. He only lived ten minutes from where he was found. Ironic, isn't it? He had a record as long as your arm, mostly small stuff dating back to juvenile. The early stuff was shoplifting and mugging old ladies' bags. He was done a couple of times for possession, but more recently for dealing. The last conviction was seven months ago. He did three months in Wakefield nick for dealing.'

'Get Jonno onto it,' ordered the DCI. 'I should think he will be able to find us a bit more about him. See if we can trace his last movements. Any sign of Lee?' Marlowe picked up his coffee and held it in both hands.

'Been back a few minutes. He's in the canteen getting warmed up,' Jenny said as she suppressed another yawn.

'Drag him out and get him to follow up on the van. Make sure it ties in with the earlier sighting and I want all the CCTV tapes of the area. Take Tanya and get down to Wood's house. Let's see if we can pull the stops out and make some real progress.'

* * *

'Leave what you're doing, Tanya. We've to go over Wood's house. I'll go and sort a car and meet you in the car park.'

Like the rest of the team, DC Etherington was knackered. She'd been staring at the computer screen through gritty eyes and getting nowhere. She saved the work she had been trying to collate and sorted herself out. Reluctantly she put on her coat, picked up her shoulder bag and headed for the car park.

The murder victim's address was only a short drive from the station and ten minutes later she pulled the pool car into the kerb outside his house which was a non-descript, mid-terraced, two bedroomed property on a post-war housing estate that had enjoyed better times. A small patch of dead earth that passed for a front garden, with a cracked flagstone path, led up to the double-glazed front door. Jenny pushed the wooden gate with the weight of her hip and kicked it clear as it scraped over the broken pavers. She fished in her coat pocket for the victim's front door key and eased it into the lock.

'Bloody hell, Tanya, it's a right tip.' the DS caught her breath as she entered the hallway and stood on the threadbare carpet. 'Be careful what you touch. We might catch something,' she added as they both took out latex gloves from their pockets and put them on. 'Let's be fair, Tan,' Jenny said as she looked through from the hallway at the debris in the lounge and kitchen, 'I did the downstairs on the last one, now it's your turn.'

Tanya turned to the DS and pulled a face. She didn't relish the thought of wading through this load of rubbish.

'Do you really think he lived amongst this?' Tanya asked as she went through to the living room, striding over the take-away and pizza boxes littering the floor.

'According to the records, he'd lived here with his mother since he was a kid,' the DS replied as she went up the stairs leading from the hallway.

Tanya surveyed the living room with distaste. The place was filthy and cramped; it was a question of where to begin. A dusty floral patterned settee took up most of the room in front of the fireplace and thin, flimsy net curtains hung at the window looking into the overgrown back garden. She decided to start on the pre-war walnut-effect sideboard. She took things out none too carefully, cast a cautious eye over everything, but found nothing.

The television stood on a low unit along with the DVD player and a stack of porno DVDs that were obviously counterfeits; probably another of his sidelines, Tanya thought to herself. Moving on through, the kitchen units were piled high with dirty pots, some encrusted with green mould. Tanya took out her expandable Asp and poked about. She didn't fancy catching some rare disease from the filth.

'How are you doing?' shouted Jenny from upstairs.

'Nothing yet, just salmonella, e-coli and a couple of spliffs in the ash tray,' Tanya shouted back as she opened and closed kitchen unit doors.

'It's much the same upstairs. Filthy.' A pile of dirty washing took up a full corner in the back bedroom. Like the downstairs, the furniture was Spartan. There were a few clean clothes in the drawers of a worn chest of drawers. A full ashtray stood on a stack of girly magazines that were piled up on the bedside table. The wardrobe was nearly bare.

111

Jenny moved on to the front bedroom, which must have been his mother's. It was still full of her things. She did a quick check of the bathroom. *Could do with a bottle of bleach in here*, she thought as she came back down the stairs into the living room.

'Jesus, there's just too much crap to sort. Best we leave it for the SOCOs to go through,' Jenny said to Tanya as she looked around. 'Come on, let's go.'

The two detectives didn't take off the latex gloves until they were outside and the front door locked behind them. Both officers peeled the tight-fitting protective gloves off their hands and dropped them into the wheelie bin.

* * *

Marlowe took the opportunity to relax for a few minutes on the small office sofa as he read the rest of the overnight reports. He could feel his head start to drop and his eyelids drooping. It had been a long night.

Sergeant Cleeves was standing outside Marlowe's office. He could see the DCI was settled with his feet on the coffee table, just about to nod off. Armed with a buff-coloured folder in his hand, he knocked loudly on the door and walked in just as the DCI's eyes closed.

'Hey up, Colombo. It's alright for some,' the Sergeant boomed out. 'There's been some bother down St. Georges. Looks like a burglary gone wrong. Some young lad got himself stabbed. He's on his way to the Hull Royal. The area car is down there now. Just going for a smoke.' Not waiting for a reply, Cleeves dropped the file in Marlowe's lap, and left.

'Bloody hell, that's all we need,' Marlowe mumbled to himself as he focused his aching eyes on the file. He glanced through the main points, then stood up and stretched himself as he walked to the doorway leading into the squad room. 'Dave, leave what you're doing and come through.'

The DI took his hands off the computer keyboard, flexed his fingers, stretched his arms over his head and yawned. The DI looked rougher from the lack of sleep than Marlowe felt, and the day wasn't anywhere near over. 'What's the problem?'

'Been a break-in and stabbing down St. Georges. Don't know all the details. As if we hadn't got enough problems. We haven't got enough bodies as it is. Trev's got a car down there. Can I leave it with you? Take Tanya with you when she gets back.'

Before the DI could respond, Marlowe had retreated and closed the office door.

* * *

Tanya had been back in the office twenty minutes, busy working on her notes of the search of the second victim's house. She glanced up when she saw the DI coming towards her work station, looking none too happy.

'Right, Tanya, grab your coat and sort out a pool car. We've got a job on down St. Georges Road. I'll meet you in the car park.'

'Just give me a couple of minutes, would you? Just want to finish these notes on the search.'

It was still freezing outside. Although the sun had turned the night into a bright morning, the frost lingered in the shaded areas. Tanya was already in the driving seat with the

113

engine running, trying to warm up the interior of the Peugeot 306, when Gowan opened the passenger door and eased his lanky frame into the car, struggling to get his long legs comfy.

'Where to, sir?' Tanya asked as she adjusted the driver's seat.

'Leonards Grove, off St Georges Road. I think it's on the left, past the railway crossing, heading for Anlaby Road.'

It was only a short drive away, a matter of minutes. There wasn't even time for the car heater to warm up properly. As they turned into the grove, they could see the area car was still on the scene outside number five. It was a tidy looking pre-war red brick house with a small fenced-in front garden. There was a uniformed officer standing by the front door who acknowledged the two detectives and led them through the hallway.

'What have we got?' Gowan quizzed him.

'The householder, Mrs Rebecca Watts, came in from work at about ten thirty this morning. Next thing she knew, this young bloke came running down the stairs, straight into her, knocked her for six and legged it. She ran out after him and saw a group of lads knocking him about in the communal garage area. Then he fell to the floor with blood everywhere.'

'Ambulance?'

'Yeah, been and gone. Should be at Hull Royal by now. He looked in a bad way.'

'Ok, thanks.' The DI walked through the shag pile carpeted hallway with Tanya close at his heels. Dave couldn't help but smile to himself and think of the DCI

114

and Shag Pile Charlie as he looked down at the floor covering. The two detectives followed the shag pile through to the living room that had a distinct overpowering sickly smell.

Gowan was shell shocked. They had gone back in time. All the furniture was sixties retro.

The DI gave Tanya a sideways Victor Meldrew, "I don't believe it," glance as he scanned the room. At one end, a vase of artificial flowers stood in the centre of a Formica drop-leaf table with plastic topped tubular steel chairs. Next to it was a semi-circular quilt-fronted cocktail bar, complete with bottle optics fixed to the wall behind it. At the other end of the room was a long, low stereogram, similar to the one Dave's mother used to have.

Mr and Mrs Watts sat in the middle of the room on what looked like a real sixties sofa. Mrs Watts was a large woman, very large, with bottle blonde hair done up in a beehive hairstyle. Her round face was heavily made up, with black eye shadow around her small squinty eyes. For such a large lady, she wore an extremely short dress, which rode up her bulky thighs. The short sleeves fitted tightly around her pudgy arms, almost tight enough to cut off her circulation. In contrast, sitting next to his wife, Mr Watts was a dapper little man of slight build, going bald, and very conservatively dressed. He looked lost as he sat with his arm around the bulk of his wife, trying to console her.

'Mr and Mrs - I'm Detective Inspector Gowan and this is Detective Constable Etherington. May we sit down?' Gowan asked, recovering his composure in this over-heated time warp.

'Of course.' Mr Watts waved them towards the two ancient armchairs placed at either side of the York stone fireplace, above which hung a print of the classic Green Lady. The room was stifling, forcing both detectives to remove their outside coats.

Tanya cleared the condensation from her glasses.

'Where do you work, Mrs Watts?' the DI asked as he turned towards the couple on the sofa.

'Smith & Nephew, the surgical appliance company on 'essle Road. You know, near the Clive Sullivan turn off. I'm a cleaner.' Everybody in Hull knew where Smith & Nephew was.

'And you came home at around 10.30 a.m. this morning, is that right?'

'Yes, that's right.'

'OK, Mrs Watts, in your own time, tell us what happened from the minute you entered the house.'

Tanya already had her notebook open to record the conversation. Dave was always pleased when Tanya was assigned to partner him; her note keeping was exemplary.

'Well, like I told them other officers, I came in at my usual time – ten thirty. I always come straight 'ome. I walked into the kitchen to put the kettle on when I 'eard this noise at the bottom of the stairs. Next thing I knew, this young bloke ran straight out of the 'allway into the kitchen. Knocked me flying, 'e did. 'E didn't 'urt me, just took me by surprise. Then 'e ran out through the back door and down the garden.'

Mr Watts kept patting his wife's arm as she spoke.

116

'What happened next?' Tanya prompted her, looking up from her notes.

'When I got meself sorted, I ran out after 'im, 'e was by the garages, in the middle of a group of lads. They was pushing 'im around. That's when it 'appened, 'e just fell down and there was blood all over.'

The heat in the room became ever more overpowering as the gas fire hissed away, Gowan slackened off his tie before carrying on. 'Did you see what happened?'

'No, I didn't,' replied Mrs Watts looking down at her pudgy hands clasped together in her lap. She wriggled her bulk into the sofa in an effort to get more comfortable and shook her husband's arm from around her shoulder.

'Did you know him?' asked Tanya.

'No, never seen 'im before.'

'In the garage area, did you see any of the lads with a knife?'

'No, like I said, I never saw no knife. They was just pushing 'im about, then he fell on the floor covered in blood.'

'What did you do then?'

Mrs Watts lifted her eyes to look at the DI. 'I came straight back and dialled 999 and went back outside again. By the time I got back, the neighbours was out. Bill from next door covered 'im with a blanket and waited with 'im until the ambulance came. I came back in and rang Steve at work, then waited on the doorstep for the bobbies.'

'Has anything been taken, Mrs Watts?'

''Aven't had a chance to 'ave a look yet,' she replied, looking towards Mr Watts.

The DI could feel the sweat starting to gather in the nape of his neck. He was longing for the interview to be over.

'And you, Mr Watts, where were you?'

'Work. Didn't know a thing until Rebecca rang me to let me know what was going on. I came straight home, didn't I, love? It was all over by the time I got here.' Mr Watts put his arm back around his wife and once again started the patting.

'Let me tell you what will happen next,' said the DI. 'Shortly someone from Forensics will be here to have a look around upstairs and in the kitchen. It's very important you don't touch anything.' The DI looked towards the uniformed constable who sat on one of the tubular chairs and nodded. 'The officer over there will take your statement and stay with you until the Scene of Crime people have finished.'

'We won't touch owt, will we, love?' Mr Watts said to his wife.

Gowan and Tanya stood up. 'That will do for now. We will want you to come into the station to give a formal statement later. In the meantime, if you do remember anything at all, tell the officer,' said Gowan.

'It's not unusual to remember some little detail when we have gone.' Tanya added as she closed her notebook and put it back in her bag. Following the DI's lead, she picked up her outside coat and hung it over her arm.

They retraced their way along the shag pile.

'Bloody hell, Tanya, could you believe that?' the DI said, shaking his head. 'I've never seen anything like it. I got the impression they would have been happier if Jack Regan from the Sweeney had turned up. Bloody woman thinks she's Dusty Springfield.'

'Who?' Tanya looked puzzled.

'Check her out on Google when we get back. You'll see what I mean.'

When they were out of earshot of the house, they both laughed aloud and headed off to have a word with the next door neighbour before returning to the station.

Chapter 12

Marlowe stood in the station car park enjoying some quiet time with a cigarette when the door opened.

'Give me a light, will you, Phil?'

Marlowe took the lighter from his pocket and passed it across to Cleavsey. The sergeant took the lighter, held it in cupped hands and lit his roll-up,

'Cheers, Phil,' he said, returning the lighter.

'How's it going with the stabbing? Anything happening with the door-to-door enquiries?' asked Marlowe.

'They're still at it. I'll let you know if anything comes up. Has one of your lads had a word with the next door neighbour?'

'Dave's on it. Anything been found at Woods' house?'

'No, not a thing. It was a bloody mess from what the lads told me. Filthy. SOCO are still down there sniffing around. We might be lucky.' The sergeant sucked on the roll-up and blew blue smoke into the air.

'Yeah, Jenny and Tanya told me pretty much the same. Has he any relatives in the area?'

'Nah, mother's in a home - dementia by all accounts - and the father walked out years ago when he was a kid.' The sergeant looked up to the sky that was now overcast. 'I hope the weather picks up a bit again. We're supposed to be going to Brid this weekend. Some concert or other, a sixties do with The Searchers.'

'They still on the go? They must be older than we are.'

Marlowe couldn't remember the last time he'd been to the seaside. Nor was he in a talkative mood. 'Have a good weekend, Trev,' he said, dropping his cigarette stub to the floor and grinding it out before returning inside.

* * *

Lee sat at his desk flicking through the mound of paperwork, searching for anything that might give him a lead on the van. Forensics had confirmed the tyre tracks had been left by a recent model Ford Transit Connect. He had the name on the van, but having spent the past two hours trying to cross-match them with the partial reg, he had come up with nothing. He was starting to think the registration plate could be false. Next was the laborious task of going through the city's CCTV, a chore he didn't relish, but knew it was vital if they were to catch the killer.

He went across to the coffee machine and came back with a cappuccino, hoping the caffeine might kick-start his brain. With his coffee by the side of his keyboard, he made a start on the CCTV tapes. His telephone rang, startling him, and over went his coffee as he made a grab for the handset. With the phone in one hand and a tissue in the other, Lee tried to clean up the mess as he spoke. 'CID. Lee speaking,' he said as he wiped at the spilt drink.

'Hi, Lee, it's Mandy from the Alliance.' It took a second or two for the name to register. 'Good morning, Mandy. How are you keeping?' Lee said, getting a vivid memory flash of her lovely smile and long legs.

'Oh, not too bad, thanks.'

'I hope you're ringing to tell me Mr Maxwell has remembered something.'

'Well, that's the thing. He hasn't come back from Ireland yet, but I have had a word with him and he remembers the man but didn't show him any premises. Is there anything else I can do for you?' It was a suggestion that threw Lee's mind into overdrive. He took a deep breath.

'Well, actually, there is. Do you fancy going out for a drink one night?' He could feel his face redden up as he spoke.

Mandy responded immediately. 'Yes, that would be nice. When are you thinking of?'

'Well, tonight's ok by me,' Lee offered hopefully.

'Ok.'

He couldn't believe his luck. Things were beginning to look up. 'I'll give you a call later to confirm, what with work and everything.'

'Ok.'

Lee returned to poring over the CCTV reports with some difficulty, but his resilience finally paid off as he spotted the Ford Transit at three locations in the city on the night in question. The young detective was feeling pleased with himself; not only had he found the suspect vehicle on the CCTV, he had arranged a date with Mandy.

* * *

'Jenny, heard any news from Karina in Forensic?' Marlowe asked over the telephone.

'I have his personal effects in front of me: wallet, some change and his mobile. The SOCOs found two folds of coke and a plastic bag with a couple of dozen ecstasy tablets in his jacket.'

'What about fingerprints?'

'There was a left hand thumbprint on one of the brass buttons on Wood's denim jacket. As yet we still haven't got a match. She found some dark woolly fibres on the plastic tape around his mouth; it could be from a jacket. If we can find the jacket, we should have enough fibres for a match.' Jenny pushed the pieces of evidence about her desk. 'Guess whose numbers are on his mobile? No prizes,' she added

'Don't tell me, the Brothers Grimm.'

'Correct. Bring them in?' she asked.

'I think you already know the answer to that one,' Marlowe replied with an edge to his voice. He immediately picked up the phone and dialled again. 'Jonno, how are you getting on?'

'I'm knackered. Nearly worn the soles off my shoes. I've done every pub around the town centre.'

'As long as you haven't had a drink in all of them.'

'Anyway, been talking to one of my informers. Told me he'd been talking to our bloke about ten o'clock. Told him he was going to head down to the Providence in St. Stephens Square to catch the trade as the kids headed into town for the clubs. I'm on my way there now.'

'Ok, call it a day after that.'

Marlowe took off his spectacles and rubbed his aching eyes with the back of his hands. He'd had enough. It had been another long day without much to show for it. The DCI turned off his computer screen and shook his head at the amount of paperwork that was mounting up again.

Some months previously, he had surprised even himself. He'd managed to use his skills of manipulation with the Super to negotiate every third weekend off, and this was one of them. He picked up a bundle of files, stuffed them into his briefcase and called it a day.

As usual when he returned home, Marlowe immediately made sure his black and white companion was fed and watered. After a meal of haddock and chips from the local chippie, accompanied by a couple of glasses of Italian Merlot, Marlowe was starting to feel human again. Once he'd had his shower, he put his outside coat on top of his towelling dressing gown and they all went out onto the Daisy's frost-covered aft deck – dog, man, cigarettes and a glass of red wine. It was a clear night once more, with a full moon that cast its glittering reflection onto the Beck. This particular night the Nokia didn't disturb the peace of the waterside and allowed him to enjoy some hours of respite.

On Saturday morning, Marlowe was up bright and early. He didn't get much chance of a lay in. Archie was always anxious to get up on deck for his constitutional. After a breakfast comprising a pot of tea, Marlowe decided on a walk into the town, only ten minutes down the towpath. With Archie on a lead by his side, he set off down the side of the Beck.

The popular market town of Beverley, like most places, was feeling the effects of the credit crunch. This was evident from the number of shut down premises and the increasing number of charity shops. However, the Saturday market area itself was as vibrant as ever. Marlowe had always enjoyed the atmosphere of the market. He bought some fresh black olives and a flat garlic bread from the Italian delicatessen stall and then moved on to browse through the second hand books. As usual, after half an hour or so he was glad to get away from the throngs of tourists meandering through the stalls. It was even worse during the summer months. He headed down Toll Gavel to Smith's Newsagents, reluctantly tied Archie's lead to one of the brass hooks outside and bought a morning paper inside. Controlling the dog with one hand and his recycled shopping bag in the other, he then strolled to his favourite café down Well Lane. A big notice on the window said, "No dogs allowed except for guide dogs".

Marlowe opened the door and had a quick glance around. Brian, the owner, was in the back and Marlowe seized the opportunity. Quickly he headed for the table at the back by the side of the stairs, the only one out of view of the counter, and installed Archie underneath the table before he was seen, tying his lead around the leg. 'Remember, keep quiet,' he told the dog. Once he was sorted out, he went to the counter and ordered a pot of tea and a toasted teacake. The plan was to spend the next fifteen minutes or so with The Independent.

The place was quite busy with tourists and locals alike, and Marlowe cringed when the Nokia tune started up in his jacket pocket. Quickly he rummaged for the mobile.

'Marlowe,' he whispered into the handset, aware of the looks from the other customers. Some even glanced down at Archie beneath the table and gave him filthy looks.

'Morning, Phil, it's Dave.'

'Oh, come on, Dave, it's my weekend off. Can't it wait?'

'Don't panic, it's not work, I've got two tickets for City this afternoon if you fancy it.'

'You're supposed to be working today,' Marlowe reminded him.

'I was. I mean I am. Dave Briggs in uniform owes me a favour. He's going to cover for me for a couple of hours.'

Marlowe glanced at his watch - plenty of time. 'Right, I'm on my way, I'll meet you at the nick.' He had another quick look around, untied the dog's lead from the table leg and headed for the door.

'See you, Phil – bye, Archie,' called Brian as they reached the doorway. Marlowe stood in his tracks and cringed, He'd been spotted again.

It was only a twenty minute walk from Gordon Street to the Kingston Communication Stadium and it was a bad outcome for Hull City. They lost 3-1 to Leeds.

Chapter 13

For the 'Nail Man', the day had been like all the other days since he'd left the hospital: boring and meaningless, with plenty of time to think and drink. The bottle of Bells whisky in front of him was down to the half full mark. In his pessimistic state he viewed it as half empty.

In contrast to the whisky, his Chinese takeaway on the coffee table in front of him was hardly touched. He didn't cook much these days; the less time spent in the kitchen the better - too many memories.

He lay back in the armchair with his legs stretched out in front of him, staring at the silent television screen. He didn't have a clue what programme he was staring at. In his right hand was another tumbler of the amber liquid. He winced as he took a large swallow and felt the alcohol burn its path all the way to his stomach. Roy Orbison singing *Sweet Dream Baby* played in the background, the words and music intermingling with the sound of his own voice going over things in his head again and again.

The first one had been the most difficult. He almost hadn't done it. But the second, that was easy and, well, the third that would be a piece of piss. *Sweet dreams*, he thought, *fat chance*. It had been a long time since he'd had sweet

127

dreams. He put the glass to his lips once more. He needed sleep even if only for a few hours.

Trying not to fall over as he stood up, he managed to get his unsteady legs to support his body, bent forward and put the glass down heavily on the coffee table. Staggering as he went, slowly putting one foot in front of the other, he managed to turn the television off as he reached for the sideboard. He was more pissed than he thought and fell forward, knocking the mini CD player onto the floor.

In an alcoholic daze, he made it to the bottom of the stairs and crawled up on all fours to the bedroom he used to share with his wife. He collapsed fully-clothed onto the double bed. His head was spinning as he lay back onto the pillow and his eyes closed. He fell asleep; sweet dreams, maybe.

It was still dark when the alcohol started to wear off and, as it did so, the dreams reappeared as vividly as ever, startling him into waking him from his stupor. As usual, he was sweat-drenched, his clothes sticking to his body. Lifting his throbbing head the best he could, he turned on his side and, through bloodshot eyes, squinted at the bedside clock. It was 5 a.m. For him it was the equivalent of a good night's sleep, even it was alcohol induced.

Realizing he was still fully dressed, he carefully manoeuvred his legs over the edge of the bed and sat with his perspiration-soaked head resting on his hands. Struggling with the effort, he managed to stand and undress, kicking his clothes into a corner. Naked, he headed for the shower.

'Soon be three nil,' he said to himself as the water cascaded over his body.

He'd nail them all.

* * *

Lee was his usual bright and cheerful self. Although he was a fastidious dresser and liked everything just so, his unruly fair hair was sticking up in every direction, looking like it could do with a comb putting through it.

He stood in front of the squad room whiteboard with a marker pen in his hand, bringing it up to date with the latest information that had come in overnight. *Precious little*, he thought.

'Is the PI in yet?' he asked no one in particular, with his back to the rest of the team.

'He's behind you,' yelled Jonno in a pantomime voice.

'Oh no he isn't,' replied Lee, still with his back to the team, keeping the theme going.

'Oh-Yes-I-Am, you cheeky bugger,' growled Marlowe from the doorway. Lee could feel the colour rising to his face in embarrassment. He wanted to crawl under the desk.

'Oh - er - morning, Boss. Just getting things up-to-date,' came the reply as he carried on with his task and tried to regain his composure.

'Morning, Lee. How did your date go with the delectable Mandy?' Marlowe let this sink in for a moment and walked further into the room. Picking up some papers and placing them to one side, he sat himself down on the corner of Jenny's desk.

'Oh, didn't think you knew. Went ok, thanks.' Once more Lee could feel the colour rising to his cheeks. He didn't dare to turn around.

'You should know by now there's nowt much goes on in this office I don't know about, even your love life. Seeing as you're already on your feet, you start us off. What's new?'

Lee had no choice but to turn around now and face the DCI. 'We got three hits on the CCTV. At 10:58 p.m., the van was picked up on the slip road at Rawlings Way heading west along the A63, Clive Sullivan Way. Then again, at 11:40 p.m., coming off at Wiltshire Road where the body was dumped at 11:46 p.m., then he drove back towards the city centre. Haven't had any luck with the number plates as yet.'

'How many people in the van?' asked Jonno.

'The pictures aren't brilliant. Couldn't get a description of the driver but there were definitely two people in the front when it was seen on Rawlings Way.'

'What about when it was spotted coming back - still two people?' Marlowe asked.

'Only one person when he's next seen coming off at Wiltshire Road. The images aren't very good, but it does match the description we have.'

'Fits in with what I was told at the Providence,' said Jonno. 'Same MO. One of the bar staff told me she saw two blokes leave at around 10:40 p.m., one half-pissed and the other helping him out. It's only a few minutes' drive to reach Rawlings Way at that time of night.'

'Well, one thing's for sure, at least we know he's familiar with the area he's operating in. It's more than likely he's a local. He either lives or works somewhere around that stretch of the Clive Sully or he has a lock-up where he does the deed.' The DCI shifted his gaze 'Jenny, have a word with Uniform and get the area car to do a street-by-street run through either side of the Clive Sully when we're done, from the town to the flyover. Have you got the post mortem results back yet?'

'Pretty much the same as the first victim. If the nail didn't finish him off, the drugs would have. Toxicology showed alcohol, heroin and Rohypnol. Karina managed to get some samples for DNA of the plastic sheeting. She thinks it could be drops of perspiration. What with the samples from the first victim, we should have enough to match up to when we find him.'

Marlowe eased himself off Jenny's desk and walked to stand in front of the whiteboard. The eight by ten monochrome prints held his gaze. Somehow, they seemed stark and alarming in comparison to the original digital colour photographs.

'OK, this is as close as we've been so far. We still have forty eight missing minutes from when the van was spotted on Rawlings Way and was next seen in the Wiltshire Road. Let's see if we can fill the gap.' Marlowe turned back to face the assembled officers, 'Thanks. Keep at it all.'

The DCI returned to his own office and poured himself a cup of coffee. With his drink in his hand, he moved across to his office window and stared through the vertical blinds into the station car park. The need to move quickly was paramount. The case was in danger of becoming stale; they needed to get a lead on the 'nail man' before he found

131

another victim, and fast, thought the DCI as he continued to stare out of the window. He moved around the desk and sat down, placed the cup in front of him, turned on his computer and picked up the telephone receiver.

* * *

The weak winter sun was shining low through the office window. Dave Gowan put his hand up to protect his eyes from the glare as he stood in front of Tanya's desk.

'What do you make of Mr and Mrs Watts?' Jenny asked as she scanned through the reports of the door-to-door enquiries.

''Odd' would be an understatement.'

'What about the next door neighbour? What's his name again?'

'Bill Withers. He's lived next door to the Watts for fifteen years. He confirmed Mrs Watts' account. He heard the commotion and came outside to see what was going on. The lad was already on the floor. He went back inside and fetched a towel and blanket, came back outside again and put the blanket over the lad and held the towel over the wound until the ambulance came. The other lads had gone when he came back.'

'What about Mrs Watts?'

'She'd gone back inside by this time,' said Tanya.

'Did he know the group of lads involved?' the DI enquired.

'All local kids. Live down the same street. Mr Withers said they were never any bother, had no problems with them. They were just a bit loud sometimes when they kicked a ball about in the car park spaces. I had a word with

132

all of them and they all told the same story. They were hanging around at the back of number five and he ran straight out into the middle of them. It was just reactions. They pushed him and he just fell to the floor. Then they noticed him bleeding. That's when Mrs Watts came running out. Any sign of the knife?'

'Uniform did a search of their homes and couldn't find bugger all. They all seem like nice kids.'

'Are any of them known to us?'

'No. Everyone the door-to-door team spoke to, said the same - nice kids, never any bother,' Tanya replied.

'Ready for a coffee?' the DI asked, taking Tanya by surprise.

'Hot chocolate please.'

Gowan walked to the vending machine in the corridor and put his money in. As usual, it threw his money back out at him. He fished around in his pocket for some different coins and eventually they were accepted. He returned two minutes later with two steaming plastic cups and sat himself on the corner of the desk.

'Thanks,' said Tanya taking one of the cups off the DI and holding it between both hands. 'Karina sent a team down and they went through the car park area with a fine tooth comb, but they came up with nothing apart from the blood on the floor. No sign of the knife anywhere. They took some fibre samples and DNA from the lads for elimination purposes and that was it. The lads are coming in later with their parents to give statements and finger prints.'

'Ask Cleevsey if he can organise a search of the gardens and bins a bit further afield. The knife must be somewhere. Don't forget the drains.' Turning to put his head away from the sun, the DI added, 'It's strange we have two conflicting reports. First off we have Mrs Watts saying the lads in the car park are little bastards, and Mr Withers and everybody else saying they are never any bother.'

'I'll tell you what else is strange. I find it hard to believe that the young lad in intensive care could have knocked Mrs Watts over. There's nothing on him. I bet he only weighs eight stone, wet through.'

'Yeah, the thought had occurred to me,' said Gowan.

'Have you heard any more from the hospital?' asked Tanya.

'Still critical as of half an hour ago. Wired up to every machine you can think of. The hospital said they would give us a ring if there is any change. Have we got a name for him yet?'

'Yeah, had a student card on him. Just a sec.' Tanya checked through her notes 'Billy Roberts. He's only sixteen, for heaven's sake. Uniform went round and had a word with the parents. The patrol car took them to the Infirmary. Word is they sat at his bedside praying for all their worth.'

'I think we should have another word with Dusty Springfield,' the DI concluded as he sipped his coffee.

Chapter 14

'Yes, sir. I know progress is slow but we are making headway. We might have a possible name for the suspect... No, sir, we haven't found him yet... Yes, sir, as soon as we have any more information I'll let you know straight away.' The Superintendent was really starting to get up Marlowe's nose

He eased back in his chair and put the telephone handset down none too gently. He then picked up the updated file on the murder investigations, flipped through it, opened his office door and walked into the squad room.

Most of the team were already out and about on their assigned duties. The exceptions were Dave Gowan and Tanya Etherington who were sitting around Tanya's desk in deep conversation, discussing the Watts case.

'Dave, I know you're still tied up with the stabbing, but Uniform have brought in the Brothers Grimm. I need you to sit in on the interviews with me.'

'No problem,' the DI replied. 'Which interview room?'

'Gary is in number one and we have Pete in number three. We'll have a word with Gary first and leave Pete stewing for a while.'

Dave stood up and ran his hands down his wrinkled suit, trying to brush away the creases.

'You look knackered.'

'No more than usual, Boss.'

'Grab some coffees and we'll have a word with Gary. Better get one for our guest.'

The red light was on above the door of the interview room to show it was occupied. Dave opened the door and Marlowe prepared himself with a big false grin on his face and walked in.

A uniformed officer was sitting on a chair in the corner nearest the door. He stood and left the room as the DCI gave him the nod. Marlowe wondered how long it would be before the room lost its Shag Pile Charlie smell. Gary Barnes sat at the far side of the Formica topped table and looked up as the two detectives entered the room.

'Morning, Gary. This is DI Gowan. I'm led to believe you've already met.' Marlowe pushed a plastic cup of coffee towards their guest.

'Cheers, Mr Marlowe.' Barnes nodded his acknowledgement to the DI. Gary Barnes had indeed crossed swords with the DI on several occasions in the past.

'This is a formal interview, Gary,' said the DCI. 'As you'll be aware, we are investigating the deaths of two drug dealers we believe are known to you. We will be taping the conversation and the video will be running. If you want to wait until your brief gets here, that's ok, it's up to you.'

Marlowe watched closely for a reaction. None came. 'No, that's ok, Mr Marlowe, I've nothing to hide.'

Bad sign not wanting his solicitor, thought Marlowe.

'You know the drill, Gary. At this time you're not under arrest and are merely helping us with our enquiries. You are free to go at any time,' Marlowe looked up from the folder he was pretending to read. A different approach was needed with Gary Barnes. He wasn't as gullible as his brother. Things had to be kept more formal. 'Do you know either of these men?' Marlowe placed photographs of the two victims on the table in front of him.

'I wouldn't say that I know them, but I have had dealings with them.'

'What sort of dealings?' asked Marlowe.

'Business, you know,' Barnes replied as he settled casually back in his chair.

'You mean they worked for you?'

'Not really worked for us. They just did the odd job now and then.'

'You really mean they pushed your drugs?'

Barnes shook his head and shrugged his shoulders in response, picking imaginary fluff from his trousers.

Dave studied the man opposite before asking the million dollar question. 'Did you have a fall out? Creamed too much off the top and you had to get rid of them?'

'Come on, Mr Gowan, what do you think I am?'

'Simple question, Gary. Did you kill them?'

Barnes put his elbows on the table and leaned forward. 'I might be a lot of things, but I'm no killer, Mr Gowan. You know me better than that.'

'What about your brother?'

Barnes shook his head in disbelief. 'You'll have to ask him that,' he replied as he picked up his coffee.

'How well did you know Gleeson?' Marlowe chipped in.

'As I've just told you, I didn't really know him. Just did the odd job for us as and when it was needed'

'Come on, don't mess us about. Was he a regular in the Sailor?'

'The only time I ever met him was on business, never for pleasure. Do I look like the sort of bloke who socializes with a little turd like that?'

It was Gowan's turn to lean across the table, looking into Barnes' eyes. 'What about the old bruises to his body. Know anything about them? Looks like the poor bugger had suffered a right kicking.' Studying Barnes' face for a reaction, he settled back in his chair, resting his hands in front of him, palms down. It looked like he'd hit a nerve.

Barnes faltered very slightly. *Better to be suspected of a beating than to be suspected of murder*, he thought to himself.

'Ah, yes, well, I can throw some light on that. We were in the city centre, you know, feeding the pigeons near the statue of Queen Victoria outside of the City Hall. Anyway, we were at the top of the steps above the toilets and he slipped. Fell all the way down, he did. Made a right mess of himself. Mind you, we looked after him. We dropped him off at the Hull Royal Infirmary.' Barnes had a challenging grin on his face.

'What about James Wood?' asked the DCI.

'Woody? Got to say I haven't seen him for about three weeks.'

'He hadn't fallen down any steps recently?'

'Nah, he's a good lad, that one. Dirty little bugger. Stinks. Have you seen where he lives? Sound one, knows what side his bread is buttered.'

'*Knew,*' corrected Gowan.

Frustration was starting to get to Marlowe. He could see they were getting nowhere. The information they were extracting from Gary Barnes was negligible. He saw no point in carrying on with the interview. Barnes was good. His script was perfect. He'd been through enough interviews over the years and knew the procedure backwards, almost as well as they did. However much he disliked the Barnes brothers, he had to admit murder wasn't their style.

'What about my brother? Have you finished with him?' Barnes asked as Dave Gowan escorted him back to the custody area.

'Don't worry, Gary, he'll be with you shortly. Have a seat and another coffee. We shouldn't be too long.'

The interview with Pete went pretty much the same as the first. He was full of shit and bravado. They came away with nothing that could help them with the investigation. Marlowe could see no further option than to release both the Brothers Grimm.

Sergeant Cleeves stood behind the custody desk as Pete was brought through to join Gary. As they were escorted to the door, Pete Barnes turned and, with a smile on his face, blew a kiss to the sergeant. Cleeves smiled back and gave him the single finger salute in reply.

* * *

'What a waste of bloody time that was,' Marlowe said to the DI as he flopped down on his office sofa.

'Mind if I use your computer?' asked the DI as he sat behind Marlowe's desk. He didn't wait for a reply. 'I wonder what Gleeson did to deserve a beating like that.'

'More than likely ripped them off. The scroat probably had it coming one way or another, I'm sorry to say. There's Jonno. Get him to come in. He might have found out something about Woods.'

Marlowe settled back, stretched out his legs and rested his head back on the cushions. Dave stood up, walked across the office and tapped on the window, gesturing for the DC to come in. He then sat once more behind the Boss' desk.

'Promotion, Dave, or just trying it out for size,' the DC quipped as he entered the office, smirking.

'How's it going?' asked the DCI as he sat forward. 'Pull up a pew.'

'Not a great deal to tell.' Jonno took off his outside coat and hung it on the coat stand. He moved a pile of files off the only other chair and put them on the edge of the desk before sitting down. 'I've been to all the usual places within about a mile radius of the town centre and nobody seems to know anything. No rumours other than it must be some nutter. Tell you what, though, I was talking to one of my informers, and he reckons the dealers are running scared, wondering who's going to be next.'

Dave lifted his eyes from the computer screen and rolled Marlowe's chair back on its castors. 'I'm not surprised. Do you think it could be turf related?'

'What, you mean like somebody trying to move into the market?' asked Jonno as he stretched his arms above his head. 'Possible, but I don't think it very likely.'

'I agree. All the reports we've had have been of a single person, I can't really see it. If it had been a lone maverick trying to muscle in, I think Gary Barnes would have tipped us off in the interview. Dave, before we knock off, have a word with Cleevsey, see if he can spare a few bodies so we can extend the search parameters.' Marlowe slammed the palms of his hands flat on his desk. 'Right, let's get on.'

Chapter 15

The temperature had dropped dramatically as the winter sun sank below the horizon. By eight o'clock it was freezing, but the town centre was already showing signs of a busy night ahead. The clans were gathering, regardless of the weather, with clusters of young men without jackets and the girls in their flimsy tops and bare midriffs, folding their arms across themselves as they huddled in groups. It would not be long before the sirens started as the police attended disturbances and ambulances took the victims away.

To be on the safe side he'd decided to leave the van in the lock-up. It was odds-on the police would be looking for it by now. He thought the best option was to use the van only on the last leg of his operations. He must have been caught on camera somewhere. He wasn't a fool. He knew about the law of averages.

The taxi pulled up halfway down Bank Side, an industrial area close to the River Hull that fed into the Humber.

When the tide was in, pleasure vessels made their way up the River Hull towards Beverley and coasters still used this stretch of the to discharge their cargoes, giving the area its own distinctive smell - a yeasty odour fused with cocoa. A hundred years ago, when the whalers returned home after a year at sea collecting their precious cargoes of whale blubber and seal fat, the smell would have been vile as the blubber was boiled down to provide oil for filling the lamps

It was only a short walk to his destination from where he was dropped off. With his collar turned up against the cold, he walked through the narrow street of disused buildings with broken windows on one side and newer custom-built units on the other. He'd already sussed out his lookout point - a deep shadowed doorway of a semi-derelict warehouse once used for the storage of corn. From his vantage point he had a good view of the pub doorway without being overlooked. He settled back into the shadows and put his hands in his pockets, then leaned back against the red brick wall and settled in for a long wait. He didn't know how long he would be there, but knew the man would come, the same as every other Thursday night.

Half an hour later there was still no sign of the man. He was sure it was getting colder. He moved deeper into the shadow of the doorway and stamped his feet to try and keep the circulation moving. Desperate for a piss, he hoped he wouldn't have to hang around much longer; his bladder was reaching bursting point. He was just contemplating going into the pub to use the toilet when he saw two men approaching.

His intended target was with another man he hadn't seen before. From where he stood it was pretty obvious a heated exchange was going on. With the hand gestures and finger pointing, the big bloke wasn't too happy. Throwing his hands in the air in a gesture of despair and turning his back on his companion, he walked through the double doors into the Sailor.

143

Two minutes later, Nail Man broke cover, crossed the short distance to the pub, and made directly for the toilet. Standing at the urinal, he sighed with relief, zipped up his fly, moved over to the basins and washed his hands. He studied his reflection in the grimy mirror. With all the trauma he'd suffered over the past months, his gaunt face and sunken eyes had the look of a user. He pushed back his lank hair with his damp hands and walked into the bar.

'Pint of bitter, please,' he ordered from the girl behind the bar.

The place was quite busy. At the far end of the bar a darts match was in progress and a domino school was under way. He stood at the end of the bar, leaning on his elbows for what seemed ages, watching his quarry. He picked up his pint, finished it off in two quick swallows and ordered another one.

When he was half way down his second pint, his heart pounding like a jackhammer against his chest wall, he made his move. He looked across at his target, picked up his pint and carefully made his way between the wooden tables across to where the man was sitting. The man didn't notice him until he stood right in front of him, blocking his view of the darts match.

'Do you fucking mind?'

Nail-man made no effort to move.

'Who the fuck are you and what the fuck do you want?' the intended victim said aggressively as he studied the man in front of him. Nail Man put his pint down on the table, pulled up a stool and sat down without saying anything.

The big bloke leaned across, looking directly into his face. 'Did I say you can sit down? I asked you what the fucking hell you want.'

The Nail Man opened his coat, put his hand in the inside pocket and produced a small bundle of ten pound notes, careful to keep it hidden from the view of those around him behind the flap of his coat.

'Ah, now I know what you want.' Pete Barnes grinned like a Cheshire cat. 'Have you got a name?'

'Tom, Dick or Harry - call me what you like, it doesn't really matter, does it?' Nail Man replied with bravado as he picked up his pint glass. He thought his heart was going to explode. The beating was so loud in his ears, he was sure the big bloke must be able to hear it.

'Couldn't give a shit one way or another. As long as you've got cash, I don't give a toss what they call you.'

It was all going as he expected. They were all the same once they saw the cash. All they could see were the pound signs rolling in the back of their eyes.

'Round the back in two minutes.' Barnes stood up and left the table. Pete knew his brother Gary would go spare if he knew he was dealing. He'd told him time and time again to leave it to the scroats but Pete could never walk away from an opportunity to make a few easy quid.

In the car park, Nail Man passed across five, ten pound notes. Barnes slipped them into the back pocket of his jeans in exchange for two plastic bags of brown powder from the inside pocket of his leather jacket. 'Nice doing business with you Tom, Dick or Harry, whoever you are.'

Nail Man gave him a nod of the head, took the brown plastic packets and put them in his pocket. 'Thanks,' he said, turning his back on Barnes and walking away.

Barnes grinned. 'Funny fucker. He'll be back, they always are,' he said to himself as he fiddled with the heavy gold chain around his neck.

Nail Man was sweating and wiped his clammy hands down the side of his coat. The hard bit was done, the ice had been broken. The next time he saw the big bloke, it would be easier. No questions would be asked.

He walked further down the one-way area of Bank Side, heading for the town centre, keeping a look out for a taxi. It was time to go home, but he didn't relish the prospect. Regardless of the elation he felt at the minute, he knew it wouldn't last further than his front door.

The dreams would still come later, regardless of how much whisky he put down his neck.

Chapter 16

Marlowe wasn't in the best of moods when he drove the Mondeo out of the compound. Once again, he'd woken up with an aching back in the saloon. Too much vino the night before was also having its effect. His temples throbbed in unison.

After a quick cup of tea, and with toilet paper stuck to his face where he'd cut himself hurrying to get shaved, he took the dog up on deck. What happened next was the final straw. As if he wasn't late enough, Archie decided to go walkabout along the Beck side, delaying him further.

Marlowe should have known the signs; it was already a bad day and about to get worse. The drive down the A1174 Beverley to Hull road was horrendous. The traffic was backed up for miles all the way through Woodmansey and Dunswell; All Marlowe could do was sit impatiently in the Mondeo watching the temperature gauge rising at an alarming rate. Once he reached the outskirts of the city, the problem refused to get any better. The congestion seemed to get worse, if anything.

Marlowe tried another tack, turning off the main road and heading for the inner city ring road and the Avenues area. Whatever the traffic problem was, it was escalating everywhere. *Time for creative thinking*, thought Marlowe, getting more stressed and frustrated by the minute.

He pulled the Mondeo into the kerb side and stopped on double yellow lines. He reached under his seat and found what he was looking for. He opened the driver's side window and stuck the blue plastic emergency light on the roof. Indicating right, he moved the Mondeo out into the traffic with the light flashing and, with heavy use of the horn, he finally made some progress as he overtook a line of cars.

By the time he pulled into the Gordon Street car park, he was well and truly pissed off, doubly so when he saw someone had nicked his parking spot. There was only one thing for it - he got out of the car, locked it and left it there in the middle of the car park, blocking everything. No one could get in and no one could get out, 'Bollocks to them all,' he shouted to the car park and the adjoining buildings at large as he walked towards the station's back door.

Sergeant Cleeves was on his regular duty on the custody desk as the DCI walked in.

'Don't even think about it, never mind say anything,' warned Marlowe. 'I've had a crap start and don't feel in the mood.' He threw down his car keys onto the desk in front of Cleeves. 'If you want it moving, move the bloody thing yourself.' He walked away, slamming the door behind him, and entered the squad room without speaking. He went straight into his office and once again slammed the door of the glass goldfish bowl. Not looking forward to what else the day would throw at him, he sat behind his desk.

DC Kristianson couldn't help but notice the DCI's arrival and the mood he was in. He left his desk, walked across to Marlowe's inner sanctum and, without hesitation, knocked on the door once and walked in.

'Guv, we've a lead on the van.'

'Guv? Where do you think this is? It's not the bloody set of the Bill, you know. You'll have to stop watching that crap. And, by the way, aren't you supposed to knock and wait to be told to come in?' This was a completely different side to Marlowe, one the young detective hadn't seen before. 'What's this about the van?'

'I finally traced the registered owner...'

'Well don't keep it a secret, spit it out,' Marlowe cut in sharply.

Lee remained calm in the face of this onslaught. 'The owner is an Ian Ball. I've got an address.'

'Is this Ball, known to us?'

Lee glanced down at his notes 'Nothing on record, not even a parking ticket.'

'Right, let's get things moving.' Marlowe stood up from behind the desk and strode into the squad room with Lee close on his heels. He walked straight to the front and stood beneath the whiteboards. 'Listen up, everybody,' he called. Immediately the room went quiet. They could sense the urgency. 'Lee's found the van we are looking for in connection with the murder investigation.' Marlowe turned to DC Kristianson 'Give us the details.'

After his bollocking, the young DC was finding it hard to put some enthusiasm into his voice. 'It took so long to find due ... '

'Never mind that at the minute.'

'Ford Transit Connect, registration number YO3 UYZ. It's registered with the DVLA to Ian Ball, 55A Hessle High Road.'

'Anything else?'

'No, Boss.' Lee replied apologetically.

'Right, this is what is going to happen,' Marlowe said as he moved into the centre of the squad room. 'Everybody, whatever you're on at the moment, put it on hold. Dave, this goes for you and Tanya too. Jonno, Tanya, you are with me.' This was the kind of excitement Tanya had joined the force for. She could barely contain herself. 'Dave, you take Jenny and Lee. Have a word with Uniform and get some extra bodies. Let me know when we are ready to go.'

Marlowe felt a twinge of guilt about the way he had spoken to TDC Kristianson. Not about to apologise, he just nodded and smiled to Lee as he left the squad room, but was ignored.

Once he was back behind his desk, he picked up the telephone handset and dialled Superintendent Bulmer's number. 'Good news, sir. We have a positive lead on the van... Yes, sir, we will be on our way shortly. Just a few details to sort... Of course, as soon as there is anything to tell you... Thank you.'

'Just about there, Boss,' Gowan called through Marlowe's open office door.

'Ten minutes in the car park.'

* * *

The place was buzzing with anticipation. Bang on time, the small convoy of unmarked police vehicles left the Gordon Street nick, heading for the A63, Hessle High Road.

The convoy passed very close to where the body was found, so close that they could see the crime scene tape along the Wiltshire Road railway lines. The traffic was light along the Hessle High Road itself as they passed through the residential area before it gave way to industrial units.

The address they were looking for was only 5 minutes from where the second body had been found. *Shouldn't do it on your own doorstep*, thought Marlowe, as the convoy of four unmarked police cars drove on towards the Sainsbury's supermarket roundabout and pulled up some 200 metres short of their destination.

Number 55A looked pleasant enough, thought the DCI. It was a post-war three-bedroomed red brick semi-detached property almost identical to the other homes along the block, all complete with double-glazing and satellite television aerials. The long front garden looked well maintained, with a low brick wall dividing it from the property next door. Although the drapes were open, the net curtains over the double-glazed UPVC windows blocked further intrusion.

Marlowe picked up his Airwave two-way radio already pre-set to conference mode that enabled all the assembled officers to listen in to what was happening. The DCI had his thumb on the press-to-talk button; DI Gowan was in the vehicle directly behind Marlowe's Mondeo.

'Dave, you take the back way. Let the Uniforms know when you are in position. I want a car on the approach road from both directions, fifty metres either side of the house.'

Gowan picked up his two-way radio and acknowledged.

Six houses away from 55A, DI Gowan could see a *For Sale* sign in the front garden. It looked ideal for their purposes. Dave, Jenny and Lee, accompanied by three uniformed constables, backtracked along the main road to the house with the sign in its garden. Once they were sure the house was unoccupied, they made their way down the gravel drive alongside the vacant property.

Jenny wondered what the asking price was. The house looked as if it had been for sale for quite a while. The long back garden was overgrown with dead grass and weeds. Keeping the noise to a minimum so as not to arouse the curiosity of any of the neighbours, they negotiated their way through the dead flora, and climbed through the bushes and over the dividing fences in turn.

Gowan went first, followed by the Uniforms. Jenny, wearing a short skirt, went last. Just as she was hitching her skirt to climb the fence, one of the Uniforms turned around. 'What! I don't need an audience,' she said as she straddled the fence and cursed as she snagged her tights on the rough wood. She could hear the officer snicker.

Painstakingly they climbed three more fences, with Jenny grumbling at each one.

The brick kitchen extension at the back of number 55A jutted out into the garden. The DI signalled to the two Uniforms to take position at the left side of the kitchen door. Gowan sneaked a glance through the corner of the

152

picture window. Jenny and Lee stood at the other side, out of sight. Gowan could see Ball sitting at the kitchen table with a cup of tea and a bowl of cereal in front of him. He seemed to be engrossed in whatever Fern Britton and Philip Schofield were discussing on the television. It was the first time Gowan was thankful for GM TV as it was keeping the man inside occupied.

'In position. He's in the kitchen,' whispered Gowan into his Airwaves radio, then, moving carefully, he backed away out of sight.

The DCI and his team waited patiently in their vehicles. Just as Marlowe was about to give the go ahead, the front door opened and a woman, who looked to be in her early thirties, came out, dressed in blue jeans tucked into wellingtons and wearing a chequered Duffle coat with the hood up. Marlowe thought it safe to presume it was the wife as she had two young children tagging along wrapped up tight in winter clothing. It was just possible to hear Mrs Ball calling out, 'See you later' as she closed and locked the door behind her. They made their way down the path.

Once the wife and children were safely out of sight, Marlowe signalled to the remaining team in the other vehicle and approached the front door. He could hear the sound from the television. He tried the door handle - the door was locked.

He banged on the glass with his fist several times and received no response. Marlowe signalled to a uniformed PC who was built like a brick shit house to come forward with the heavy metal door enforcer. The officer swung the battering ram into the lock of the double-glazed door. The door shattered and flew freely in the frame on the first attempt. *So much for security locks*, thought Marlowe. He shouted, 'NOW!' into the two-way radio.

In unison, both teams rushed into the house, Marlowe first, closely followed by Jonno. They made it to the kitchen just as Gowan entered through the rear door.

Ball could not believe his eyes. He hadn't a clue what was happening as his home was invaded by police officers. He just sat there open-mouthed with his spoon in his hand.

'Don't move, Mr Ball,' Marlowe said as he entered the kitchen. 'Just stay where you are.'

One of the uniformed officers stood behind Ball with his hands on his shoulders. 'You do not have to say anything. But it may harm your defence if you do not mention, when questioned, something which you may later rely on in court. Anything you say may be given in evidence.'

Ball still sat in the same position, totally non-plussed as the officers spread around the house. One officer stayed by the front door as Jonno went upstairs, putting on his latex gloves as he went.

'Lee, go and check the garage. See if the van's there.'

TDC Kristianson pushed his way out the back way while Tanya headed for the dining room to search for evidence. Dave and Jenny started to go through the kitchen units and drawers.

'What the hell's going on?' Ball yelled at the top of his voice.

'My name is Detective Chief Inspector Marlowe. We have reason to believe you are connected with two recent murders. We have a warrant to search the premises.'

Marlowe threw the warrant down on the kitchen table and turned back to Ball, scanning the kitchen. 'Turn that bloody television set off,' he ordered a uniformed constable.

'Murder? Are you having a laugh? I don't know anything about any murders.' With a rapidly paling face, Ball looked around the room at the officers.

'Where's the van, Mr Ball?' asked Gowan, standing directly opposite him.

Ball remained at the table. His heart was pumping and his face had turned ashen with fright. 'What van?' His eyes searched the DI's face.

'Your van, Mr Ball. You are the owner of a dark blue Ford Transit Connect, registration number YO3 UYZ?' Marlowe could hear the searching officers opening drawers and cupboards upstairs and in the living room.

'Yes. I mean I was.' Ball answered, his frightened eyes staring at Gowan.

'What do you mean 'was'?' Marlowe could feel his face start to flush.

'I sold it on e-Bay about three months ago.'

Wrong answer. *Oh shit*, Marlowe thought. He couldn't believe his ears.

'You what!' The atmosphere in the kitchen was intense. The DCI could feel the colour creeping up his neck to his face. Subconsciously he clenched and un-clenched his fists by his side. He looked into Gowan's face, then back at Ball. 'Who did you sell it to? Have you got a receipt?' Marlowe knew he was on the way to a kicking. 'You do know it is an offence not to notify the DVLA of a change of ownership?' Marlowe could not believe what he had just said - a full team of officers, complete with body armour, running amok around the house and the only offence Ball had committed was not notifying the DVLA of a change of ownership. DCI Philip Marlowe hadn't felt such a prat since he was a probationer a lifetime ago.

'Get the details, Inspector Gowan,' he growled, turned his back and walked out of the house into the front garden, slamming the door behind him. The shattered door lock and catch had no chance of holding and it sprang back, bouncing off the doorframe.

Out in the garden he was more pissed with himself than anything else. He stood by the front gate and fastened up his coat. He dug deep into his pocket for his cigarettes and pulled out the packet of Bensons. With his hands slightly shaking, he pulled one loose from the packet. He put the filter tip between his lips and cupped his hands against the wind as he flicked his lighter, putting the flame to the cigarette. It was still blowing a gale outside. He took a deep drag of the cigarette and screwed up his eyes as the wind blew the blue smoke into his face. What had started as a bad day was rapidly becoming the day from hell.

* * *

Cleeves knew when to take the piss and when not to. Although he was a pal of Marlowe, he waited until the DCI and Gowan had passed through his custody area before laying into the rest of the team.

'Well, well, well if it's not Hannibal Smith and the 'A' Team. Sorry, I meant the Keystone Cops.'

If looks could kill, Jenny would have murdered him then and there.

* * *

The bar in the George was busy by the time Dave and Jenny walked in. A boisterous ladies' darts match was taking place.

'What are you having?' Dave asked with his mouth close to Jenny's ear as they pushed their way forward.

'White wine spritzer, please.'

'Pint of lager and a spritzer,' Gowan shouted to the barmaid above the noise. Gowan paid for the drinks and pointed to a table as far away from the ladies' darts teams as possible. The small round table, right next to the toilets, wasn't ideal. Jenny took off her coat and hung it on the back of the chair.

'Swap seats?' asked Gowan.

'Come off it, I've just sat down,' said Jenny as she picked up her glass.

'Come on, it's that old gadger over there, the one I was talking to the other night. If he sees me, I'll never get home once he starts with the stories.'

Reluctantly Jenny traded places with the DI. 'Did you see the PI's face when Ball told him he'd sold the van?'

'Talk about having the wind knocked out of your sails. I thought he was going to have kittens,' Gowan replied as he licked the froth from his lips.

'And when he said it was an offence not to report the sale to the DVLA. Poor bloke couldn't believe it with us lot togged up in stab vests.'

They both laughed unrestrainedly at the thought.

Gowan finished his pint and stood up. 'Are you having another?'

157

'No thanks. I'm going to make tracks. I thought you were going to see Joan and the kids.'

He shrugged his shoulders, 'It's not that I don't want to see them. I just can't face the old dragon they live with.'

Gowan edged his way through the crowd and made his way back to the bar while Jenny put her coat on.

'Hey up, how ya doin', young-un?' The old gadger had collared him. Gowan knew he was in for a long night.

Jenny fought her way past the ladies' darts teams, turned and shook her head at Gowan as she left the pub.

* * *

'Well, Archie, at least you're glad to see me,' Marlowe declared as he bent down to pat the dog scampering around his legs. 'It looks like you've had a better day than I have.'

Once his companion was fed and watered, Marlowe took a bottle of Spanish Shiraz from the wine rack, went through to the saloon and slumped down in the dinette. The thought of a nice glass of vino had kept him going.

He took a file from his battered briefcase and tried to give thought to the day's catastrophic events. He was struggling. If he was being honest with himself, he just couldn't be bothered.

Marlowe dropped the file on the table and swapped it for the wine as the more promising of the two options. The Shiraz soon had a mellowing effect on him and he discovered he was hungry. He went through to the galley and looked in the fridge. He settled on a piece of ageing Cheddar cheese and some biscuits. He couldn't be bothered to mess about with cooking.

Feeling slightly better with himself, Marlowe put on his shoes and coat. As soon as the dog saw this, he began running in between Marlowe's legs excitedly. The DCI didn't want a repeat performance of the morning's events and slipped Archie onto his lead. With the dog lead in one hand, a poop scoop and plastic bag in the other, he climbed the three wooden steps up from the galley onto the aft deck.

He stood on the Beck side in the cold night, smoking a Benson's, watching the moon shimmering on the still water. He was determined to make it to his bed tonight.

Chapter 17

Tanya knocked on the green wooden door down St. Leonards Grove. Almost immediately the door opened. The bulk of Mrs Watts filled the doorframe, her and her piled-high Bee Hive hairdo. The DC had Googled 'Dusty Springfield' on the internet to see what Gowan had been going on about. She couldn't help but smile inwardly as the door opened.

'Mrs Watts, remember me? DC. Etherington?'

'Of course I do, luv. Come on in.'

The bright red, pursed lips hardly moved as she spoke.

'And what can I do for you?' She nodded towards the fireside armchair for Tanya to sit. 'Please, call me Becky.'

Tanya ignored the request. 'I just have another couple of questions about the incident, if you wouldn't mind.'

"Dusty" lowered herself with some difficulty into the chair opposite Tanya.

'Going back to the day in question, you arrived home at what, ten thirty?'

'That's right, dear.' She again sat with her pudgy hands clenched in her lap, Tanya noticed.

'We need to get things in order. You called the police as soon as the incident happened, is that right?'

'Like I told you before, I'd only been in a couple of minutes when 'e ran down the stairs, through the lounge and straight out the back way.'

The room was stifling hot, as it had been on her previous visit with the DI, and had the same sickly lingering odour. Tanya ran her fingers around the neck of her sweater to try and let some air circulate. She didn't know how such a large lady could stand the heating turned up that much. 'Did you call your husband before the police and ambulance?'

'To be honest, I can't rightly remember.' She hesitated slightly. 'Must 'ave rung 'im after.'

When Mrs Watts used the phrase 'to be honest', Tanya immediately doubted she was hearing the truth. 'And Mr Watts, where is it he works?' she asked, consulting her notes.

'Only around the corner at Fast Print, 'e's the manager, you know.' She was obviously proud of her husband's position. 'Would you like a cup of tea, luv?' She sat forward on the edge of the chair.

Tanya shook her head. She didn't want to spend any longer than necessary in this retro sweatbox. The eyes of the green woman in the picture over the fireplace seemed to be staring at her. 'How long did it take him to get home after you called?'

'Like I said, 'e's in charge and 'e can come and go. 'e came straight away, only took two minutes.'

'Thanks very much for your help, Mrs Watts. I think that will do for now.'

Tanya stood up and put her notebook away in her shoulder bag and Mrs Watts showed her out into the hallway. 'Do you mind if I go out the back way?'

Tanya didn't wait for a response and walked straight into the kitchen, checking it out in relation to the stairs the victim was supposed to have come from. 'Well, thanks again, Mrs Watts. We'll be in touch.'

Mrs Watts smiled at the detective and closed the door.

The cold air was a relief after being sat in front of a hissing gas fire. Tanya took a deep breath of fresh air. She was having a problem with the sequence of events. It had been niggling her since their initial visit to the house. The times didn't quite fit.

* * *

Tanya's stomach was making loud growling noises. She had missed breakfast and was starving by the time she returned to the station. She was just tucking into a healthy pre-packed snack of fresh pasta and green salad when Dave Gowan came across. 'How's it going?'

Tanya shrugged her shoulders as she dabbed her lips with a paper napkin. 'I don't know what it is, really. Something just doesn't seem quite right. She has everything off pat, so to speak. Can't get the times right in my head.'

'Get in touch with the Duty Officer in the control room. Ask for a report of when the 999 call was logged. Check again with the next door neighbour on his times and also check with her employer. She must have signed out or clocked off.'

'Good idea. Think you could ask Karina in SOCO to send someone around to have a good look at the kitchen?'

162

'Shouldn't be a problem.' He started to move over to his own desk to organise it when he turned back towards Tanya. 'What about that smell in the living room? What did you make of it?'

'Why, what do you mean?'

'Well, you said you don't think they are quite what they seem. Someone could have been busy cleaning what they didn't want seen. You never know. I'll ask Karina to look into it when they check the kitchen.'

First things first, thought Tanya, and dug her fork once again into her lunch as the DI returned to his paperwork.

* * *

Marlowe was feeling more frustrated than ever as he sat behind his desk waiting to be summoned by the Super. It had to come. A major bollocking was expected.

He leaned back in his chair, took off his spectacles and dropped them on the ever-growing pile of paperwork. He screwed up his eyes and rubbed them with his knuckles. By now his head was throbbing something fierce. He reached out, opened the top desk drawer, and took out a packet of Paracetomol. *Lack of sleep and too much Merlot*, thought Marlowe.

The DCI pressed two tablets from the blister pack and grimaced as he swallowed them back with what was left of his cold coffee. He shook his head in disgust and returned the packet to the drawer. He picked up the telephone. 'Jenny, come through, will you?'

It was only seconds before Jenny appeared. Marlowe nodded his head towards the chair opposite and the DS sat down. The DCI leaned forward with his elbows on the desk

163

and rested his chin on clenched fingers. 'How's it going out there? All the jokes finished with?'

'Didn't last long, Boss. It's forgotten, for now.'

'To be expected, I suppose. Can't see the funny side of it myself yet.' Marlowe smiled for the first time in twenty-four hours as he put his spectacles back on. 'After yesterday's cock-up - my cock-up - things have to start happening. We need progress. Tell everyone to make sure their notes are up-to-date.' Marlowe glanced up at the wall clock; it was already 3.30 p.m. 'I want a briefing in the squad room in an hour.'

* * *

By 4.30 p.m. everyone was assembled in the squad room, waiting.

'What a cock-up! Couldn't organise a piss up in a brewery,' said one of four extra uniformed officers assigned to the team for the duration. 'Makes you wonder if he might be better off as a PI instead of a DCI.' His colleagues sniggered. Most of the regular team took no notice, all the same Jenny shot him a look, and the officer immediately shut up just as Marlowe came in.

'Ok, let's make a start.' He moved to stand beneath the whiteboards, which were now looking cluttered. 'Jenny, start us off.'

'Forensic confirm DNA other than the victim's was found in both instances. Checks on the database haven't revealed any matches on record.' Jenny remained sitting behind her desk. 'The first victim's leather jacket was covered in prints, but none matched the partial print on the brass button on the second victim's denim jacket. We're still waiting. Apart from that, we're struggling.'

164

'Tell me about it. Any further leads on the van, Lee?'

'Sorry, Boss. Whoever bought the van off Ball has failed to register the change of ownership,' Lee replied as he waited to be rebuked by DCI Marlowe. Nothing came. Marlowe was still feeling a little guilty about the way he had taken his frustration out on the young TDC the day before. 'Technical has enhanced the video of the van when it was picked up on Hessle Road. Definitely two people. The guy in the passenger seat is the second victim, no question about it. The bad news is you can't make out the driver and there have been no further sightings of the van.'

'Has anyone any new information they want to share with the rest of us?' asked the DCI. There was no response. 'Ok, let's try and see if we can make any sense of this mess.' Marlowe turned to face the board behind him. 'Two victims - did they know one another?'

'Probably. They were in the same line of business,' Tanya answered.

'We do know it's the same MO and they are definitely connected. There's no doubt about that. The same person murdered them both. Motive... what are we missing, anyone?'

Jenny again jumped in. 'Definitely not robbery. Both victims still had their wallets intact. He left their mobiles. Both were low level dealers and he filled them full of crap before he finished them off. Got to be drug related.'

'I'll go along with that, but we're still missing a motive,' replied the DCI.

Lee looked across at Jonno. 'You still don't think it's a new team in the area, making themselves known?'

Jonno shuffled the papers in front of him and pushed back his chair onto two legs. 'No, a few broken bones, maybe, but this is too aggressive, too well planned.' Jonno let the chair drop back onto four legs. 'Besides, it would have been all over the city by now and we'd have seen a lot more activity from the Brothers Grimm. The big question is, is he working alone?'

The DCI turned to the mouthy uniformed officer. 'I want you and your oppo to go over the CCTV from both cases again. Look further afield. Something might have been missed.' Mouthy and his mate rolled their eyes as the DCI looked away.

'Jonno, go home and get your head down for a couple of hours, then do the trawl around the usual places. Someone may be icing something back. See what you can turn up.' Marlowe noticed a slight smirk on Lee's face. 'You can take Lee with you.' The young TDC's face dropped a mile; he'd have to cancel his date with the delectable Mandy. 'Jenny, re-read the reports and statements. See if we have missed something and collate what we've got so far.'

'Already started, Boss,' said the DS, leaning across her desk as she arched her aching back.

'What do you want us to do, sir?' asked one of the remaining constables leaning with his back on the wall, his pen poised over his notebook.

'First thing in the morning I want every lock-up on Hessle Road checked for the van, side streets, the lot. We know he was looking for a workshop at one point. Do the obvious ones first, un-occupied, ones with To-Let signs, etc.'

166

Marlowe sat on the corner of Jonno's desk. 'That's it folks. Let's call it a day and start again in the morning.'

The DCI stood and stared, giving the whiteboard one more glance before returning to his own office. He sat behind his desk and read the emails that had arrived while the briefing was taking place, then, as there was nothing that couldn't wait until the morning, he opted to have another half an hour catch-up with his paperwork while it was quiet.

* * *

By the time Jonno and Lee met up again later that evening in the Brass Bull, the weather had changed again; it was beginning to snow. Everywhere was white over. Lee was prepared. He was wearing his expensive black overcoat that reached down to his knees.

'What are you wearing?' Lee asked Jonno with a broad grin on his face. Jonno was dressed in jeans and a camouflage jacket over a Bryan Adams tee shirt with white trainers on his feet.

'Not my idea. The wife said if I was going on the town with you, I should look the part. Trendy, she said you would be,' Jonno replied, wishing he could go home and get changed into something more conservative. 'The wife bought the tee shirt when she went to a concert at the K.C. Stadium. Pretty cool, don't you think?' He burst out laughing as they fought their way to the bar. 'What are you having?'

'Just a coke, please, I've come in the car.' Lee looked around. It was busy were a few free tables. They took their drinks and sat on stools at a pitted copper-top table.

'How are you finding CID?' asked Jonno.

'Like your tee shirt, pretty cool,' he answered, smiling.

'How long are you with us?'

'Depends on the PI. I'd like to think it could be permanent, but, the way things are going, I wouldn't be surprised if I am on my way out. He gave me a right gob full the day before yesterday.'

'Don't worry about it, son. He has a go at us all from time to time,' Jonno said as he looked around the bar checking to see if any of his informers were in. 'I remember the time when - hang on, we need to have a word with that bloke who's just come in.'

Jonno and Lee picked up their drinks, walked to the end of the long bar and stood at either side of the newcomer.

'Oh no, come off it, Jonno, not tonight. I just want a nice quiet drink and a game of arras. You've come mob-handed, I see.' He glanced towards Lee.

'Only a quickie, Sammy. This is my mate Lee.' Lee nodded, pulled two black and white photographs from his inside pocket and put them down on the bar in front of Jonno's snout, carefully avoiding any damp patches. 'How about these two? What can you tell us?'

'Don't know him,' he said as he pushed away the picture of Gleeson, the first victim. 'Know this one, though.' He tapped his finger on the black and white photograph. 'Jim Wood. Everybody calls him 'Woody'. Dirty sod, stinks to high buggery. Got B.O. or something real bad.'

'Anything else other than his hygiene problem, and, by the way, I should say he did stink. Sadly, he's not with us anymore.' Lee picked up the photographs and returned them to his pocket.

'Think he lived somewhere around the North Road area. He usually worked in the Old Town - Whitefriargate, High Street and down Princes Dockside, those areas. Can I go now?'

'In a minute. Anything else?'

'Small-time, really. Pills, a few e's and stuff like that. There's a good market on student nights. So they tell me,' he added so as not to incriminate himself.

'What about this bloke. Seen him?' Lee showed his a computer-generated likeness of the suspect.

'Nah, can't say I have.' Sammy shook his head as he took another look. 'What's he been up to?'

'If I told you, we'd have to kill you. Cheers, Sammy, we'll leave you to it.' Sammy nodded, picked up his pint and headed across to the dart board. 'By the way, who got you ready to come out?' Sammy jibed as he walked away, laughing.

'Piss off,' fired back with a smile on his face. 'Well, that was a lot of good. Let's have a quick word with the bar staff before we move on.'

'Bloody hell, have a look out here.' Jonno moved clear of the pub doorway, keeping to one side, allowing Lee to stick his head out of the door.

'Looks like your trainers are going to get wet,' said Lee as he stood in the doorway, watching the snow thicken on the pavement beyond. 'Right, where to next?' He buttoned up his coat and pulled his coat collar up as they both stepped out into the snowy maelstrom, which was whipping up.

Chapter 18

Eight tubular steel chairs stood arranged in a semi-circle on a short-piled green industrial carpet. Colourful reproduction Monet prints, hung on three of the institutional beige coloured walls, did little to brighten the room. Behind the chairs, patio doors looked out onto a well-kept garden area. The sun was shining through, warming the backs of the occupants of the chairs who sat in various states of dress; a mix-and-match of oddments of clothing, tracksuits, pyjamas and dressing gowns.

Each and every one of the occupants was different. Some were voluntary patients, while others had been sectioned. One thing they had in common was they all had a different tale to tell.

He remembered them clearly because he was one of them.

It was his second visit to the group therapy session. He remembered a young bloke with a spotty face rocking back and forth on his chair. The bugger wouldn't stop; it really pissed him off. A young, slightly-built female psychologist sat in front of the group. Her thin, pale face was shrouded with long dark hair hanging down over her face. Her fringe was hanging to one side, almost obscuring her right eye. He thought she could have been mistaken for a patient if not for the fact she sat at the front with a clipboard across her knees. She was so young she looked as if she should still have been at school. Her gaze travelled from one to the other, then she looked in his direction and fixed his eyes with hers.

'How are you feeling today?' she asked in an over-sympathetic tone, her hands clasped in her lap as they rested on her clipboard. He remembered staring at her as if he could see right through her body. 'How are you?' she repeated. *So patronizing*, he thought.

He suddenly realized the question was being directed towards himself. He shifted his gaze, and focused on the one eye he could see. 'How do you think I'm feeling?' he said, answering her with another question.

'I know you must be feeling sad,' she replied.

'Do you?' This was it; he couldn't listen to any more. 'You really think so!' The young psychologist nodded in response. 'You know how I must be feeling, do you? Did your filthy rotten drugged-up son die, choking on his own vomit and lying in his own piss?' He could feel the eyes of the entire group staring. 'Oh yes, I nearly forgot, that was after he smashed his mother's - my wife's - head in with my fucking hammer!' The crazy in the group sniggered. 'You silly little girl, how can you possibly know how I'm feeling?' He stood and the tubular chair fell over as he walked out of the room and slammed the door behind him.

That was the last time he went to a group session.

Naked, he stood staring at the gaunt reflection peering back at him in the bathroom mirror. The new hair clipper buzzed and vibrated in his hand. He brought it up to his head, stared into the mirror and started ploughing lines

171

across his head. Black strands fell into the bathroom basin, clogging around the damp chrome drain hole. He kept going with the vibrating machine, back and forth, until his head was free of hair, and stubble covered his white scalp.

He smiled to himself at the memory of his wife. She'd always been going on at him to change his hairstyle but he didn't think she would have meant for it to be this drastic. He turned the clippers off and put them down on the vanity basin. He looked in the mirror once more. He hardly recognised himself. If he couldn't recognise himself, it was very unlikely that anyone else would.

He turned on the power shower and waited for steam to fill the cubicle. He stepped in and slid the door behind him. The hot water of the shower revived him to some extent as it cascaded down his body, rinsing away the loose hair that clung to him. Free from wisps of newly mown hair, he wrapped a towel around his waist and went back through to the bedroom, let the towel drop to the floor and dressed. Tonight he chose something different to match his new image: faded jeans - not fashionably so, just faded with age, and the same applied to the sweatshirt he pulled over his head.

Once he was finished, he went back downstairs to the living room and took the bottle of Bells from the sideboard. He filled a tumbler half full with whisky and raised it to his mouth. The whisky burned a path from his throat to his stomach as he swallowed half the measure in one, the fire of the alcohol making his eyes water. He wiped them with the back of his hand and topped up the glass. Crossing the room, he switched on the television set with the volume turned down, then dropped onto the sofa and stayed there until it was time to go. Maybe tonight, maybe not, but sometime soon he'd achieve a just reprisal.

Chapter 19

'Morning, Tanya,' Gowan greeted her as he entered the squad room with a plastic cup of coffee in his hand. 'You're in bright and early.'

The DI took off his coat and hung it over the back of his chair. He walked across to Tanya's desk, taking his coffee with him. 'Anything I should know about?'

'Good news or bad news? Which do you want first?' Tanya asked as she looked up from the computer screen.

'Let's start with the good. It's about time we had some.'

Tanya took off her spectacles and gave them a rub with a tissue, 'I've just heard from the hospital. Young Billy Roberts is out of intensive care. Uniform have been and had a word with him.' She put her spectacles back on.

'Brilliant!' The jubilation showed on Dave's face.

'Now the bad news. He can't remember bugger all. He remembers standing in the Watts' living room and next thing he knew he was in the ambulance. The Doc reckons he banged his head on the concrete when he fell. Concussion.'

'Bollocks, so we're not much further on.' The DI slammed the palm of his hand down on the desk. 'Shit.'

'Don't get stroppy, there's more,' said Tanya. She had the DI's interest again. 'I had a word with Karina as I came in. She's just about finished her report on the Watts' house. She said to give her ten minutes and she'll come through.'

'I hope it's better bloody news than you gave me,' the DI mumbled just loud enough for Tanya to hear.

She rolled up the tissue she had been using to clean her spectacles and threw it at the DI, narrowly missing his coffee.

* * *

'Morning, Columbo.' Cleeves said as Marlowe walked in from the car park.

'Good morning to you, Trevor.' This knocked the Sergeant for six. He wasn't used to the DCI being polite at this time of the morning.

'Still snowing out there?' asked the Desk Sergeant.

'Still at it,' Marlowe replied as he shook the snow off his shoulders. 'It's worse in Beverley. I opened the hatch doors and a bloody avalanche came in. Had to dig Archie out.' They both laughed, Marlowe thought it funnier than Cleeves. The DCI was still chuckling to himself as he walked into CID. 'Morning all,' he said as he entered the squad room and was answered by the usual early morning grunts and groans. 'Anything new overnight, Dave?'

'Nothing out of the ordinary, Boss. Not snowed in, then?'

'Very nearly.' The perfect opportunity. Marlowe went on to tell his avalanche story again before he went into his office.

Wearing a smart black trouser suit, Karina from SOCO was next to enter the CID squad room. Her own office was on the third floor. She went straight across to the DI's desk and put down the buff folder she had brought with her. As

175

soon as Tanya saw her come in, she left her desk and walked over to join them.

'Good news, I hope, at least better than Tanya's effort.' Gowan looked across at the DC.

'It's that good you will be buying me drinks for a week,' Karina said as she brushed away a stray blonde hair from her face. 'First of all, the smell in the living room, it was industrial carpet cleaner. It had been used to wash away whatever was spilt on the carpet. Nothing showed on the surface but Mrs Watts had a duck fit when I started pulling bits of strands out of the carpet. Anyway, regardless of her mouthing off, I brought a sample back to the lab with me. You're going to like this. Guess what. Go on, have a guess.'

'She bought it from Shag Pile Charlie?'

'Ha ha, very funny. We found blood traces in the backing weave. Someone had tried to wash away blood.'

'Brilliant, Karina.'

'I know I am,' the SOCO replied.

'Anything else?' asked Tanya.

'Not in the living room. You remember the kitchen had laminate flooring? Well, again, we found traces of the same bleach-based floor cleaner. People always wipe surfaces clean, but forget about the joint between the boards. Anyway, I took some scrapings and guess what. Yes, no prizes for guessing - more dried blood. DNA tests should confirm they are a match to the victim.'

'Karina, you're a star. Never mind drinks for a week, we'll make it a month. Tanya will stump up as well!'

Tanya looked at the DI with an open mouth but no sound came out of it.

'You're welcome,' said Karina. 'In that case I'll see you both in the George tonight. Don't forget your wallets.'

'Well, you know what to do next, Tanya,' Dave said with a broad smile on his face. 'You'd better take a couple of uniforms with you when you pick Mr and Mrs Watts up. Don't want her bashing you about. She's a big lass.'

* * *

DCI Marlowe stood looking out of his office window. The snow was falling steadily and lay in a thick white carpet in the car park. He could not help but give a thought to Gazzer, the homeless man, living in his make-do shelter. Marlowe shivered involuntarily at the thought of living in a home made from cardboard boxes, and turned away. With his back to the window, he leaned back on the radiator, resting the palms of his hands on the top of the warm metal.

'How did you two get on last night?'

Lee and Jonno sat down as Marlowe nodded towards the small sofa. Simultaneously both officers shook their heads.

'Bugger all. Apart from getting frost bite, nothing that we didn't know already,' reported Jonno. 'We showed the identikit picture around and, yes, one or two said they had seen someone who resembled the picture but nothing definite. Nobody seems to know him.'

'All-in-all, we didn't have any luck,' added Lee.

'Do you still think he's a local?' Marlowe directed the question to Jonno.

'Yeah, well, I did think maybe he or she came down the M62, did the job and then disappeared. I mean, with the second victim being from Leeds. But saying that, when you look at the CCTV of the M62 between here and Leeds, the

177

van doesn't show on either night in question, so that kicks my theory into touch. Yes, I'd put money on it, he's a local.'

'Ok, thanks, lads.' Marlowe dismissed the two officers. He'd had the same thoughts himself - out of town or local? He poured himself another mug of thick coffee before he reluctantly started to wade through the mountain of paperwork. The in-tray on the edge of his desk was mounting up alarmingly each day the murder investigation remained unresolved.

* * *

The heat coming out of the interview room was stifling. DI Gowan could smell the new paint still burning off the radiators. *Bloody hell, they get younger*, thought Gowan as he walked into the interview room and saw the young uniformed constable sitting quietly on a chair in the corner nearest the door. Gowan nodded his thanks and the constable left the room as he and Tanya sat themselves down at the Formica table opposite Mrs Watts. "Dusty" just sat there looking lost while the detectives got themselves sorted.

Gowan closed up the manila folder, picked it up and made a conscious effort of tapping the edges square on the table before he made eye contact with their guest. 'Good morning, Mrs Watts. Thank you very much for coming in.'

Mrs Watts was dressed as usual in her black retro miniskirt and was additionally wearing a bright red turtle-neck sweater, which hugged her bulges. The red of the sweater was exactly the same colour as the lipstick on her thin, pouting lips. Even her feet seemed to bulge from the sides of her red platform shoes. Dave and Tanya found it

178

difficult not to stare as her mini skirt began riding up the ample bulk that was overhanging the plastic seat. Tanya, who only weighed eight stone, couldn't help but think how uncomfortable this must have been.

The two officers sat quietly, seemingly scanning through their notes, giving "Dusty" time to think about what she was going to say.

'That's alright, but I don't know what I can tell you that you don't know already,' she said as she sat awkwardly, looking at them with her heavily made up piggy eyes.

'That may be, but a few things have come up in the course of our enquiries that need clearing up. But first my colleague, DC Etherington, is going to read out a caution, then we are going to record our conversation.'

When Tanya had finished, Mrs Watts remained quiet and began fidgeting with her handbag, which she was holding on her knees.

'Do you understand what my colleague has said?' asked the DI.

'Yes, I think so.' Her pudgy fingers with chipped nail varnish dipped into her bag and she produced a tissue that she proceeded to dab her nose with.

'Before we go any further, do you want a solicitor present? If you don't have one, we can get you the duty solicitor,' suggested Tanya.

After a lengthy pause she replied, 'Yes please, dear. I think that would be best. Will you let my husband know?'

Tanya turned off the tape machine and suspended the interview. 'If you would wait here with the constable, please,

Mrs Watts, we'll let you know when your solicitor arrives. In the meantime, if you need anything, just ask the officer.'

Mrs Watts nodded and sniffed into her soggy tissue. Dave and Tanya left "Dusty" in the stifling room and closed the door behind them. They were thankful for the cooler air in the corridor.

'Good sign,' said the DI when they were back in the corridor.

'Maybe,' replied Tanya. 'Best not get too excited yet.'

'Let's grab a bite to eat in the canteen while we have chance.' However, before they had made it to the stairs leading up to the canteen, Marlowe came out of the squad room, scratching at his neck.

'How are you getting on in there? Any good?'

'Nearly there, Boss. Waiting for her solicitor to arrive,' replied Tanya.

'Could do with some good news,' said Marlowe as he disappeared into the custody area for a word with Sergeant Cleeves

Twenty minutes later, after a cheese roll and two cups of coffee, Tanya and Dave went back to carry on with the interview. This time Mrs Watts was accompanied by Mr Alvin Brocklebank, the duty solicitor.

Brocklebank, built like a beanpole, sat by her side with his notepad on the table in front of him, chewing the end of his pen, with his knees banging under the table. The duty solicitor always surprised the DI. Even in this weather he'd come on his mountain bike and managed to look smart.

The heat in the interview room was overpowering, nearly as overpowering as Mrs Watts' sickly perfume. Tanya and Dave sat down and Tanya re-started the tape recorder, announced the time and listed the people present in the room. The tape machine hummed quietly in the background.

'Mrs Watts,' said Tanya as she looked up from her notes, 'you arrived home from work at 10.30 a.m., is that correct?'

Mrs Watts nodded.

'For the benefit of the tape, Mrs Watts nodded her head in agreement,' Dave said quietly, trying not to make "Dusty" feel uneasy.

'Did you make any phone calls before you rang 999?'

'No,' she replied, looking down at her hands.

'What happened next?'

Mr Brocklebank sat fiddling with his ear lobe, nodding towards his client.

'I've told you all this before. It just felt as if something was wrong, know what I mean?' Mrs Watts looked towards her solicitor for support, Brocklebank nodded for her to carry on. 'Anyway, I went into the kitchen and then I heard a noise. Next thing I knew 'e was running through the kitchen. Knocked me for six, 'e did.'

'And?' said Gowan.

'Well, he just ran out the back door. Next thing he was on the floor after one of them lads stabbed him.'

'What happened next?' asked Tanya as she looked up from the file on the table in front of her.

'I came in and dialled 999.' Mrs Watts looked uncomfortable in the heat of the interview room. The perspiration was glistening on her top lip above the red lipstick. The two detectives remained silent for what seemed like an age. Mrs Watts looked back and forth between their faces, and then to her solicitor as they remained quiet.

'What I don't understand, Mrs Watts, is we checked your home phone records and contacted your mobile provider. It appears you rang your husband before you rang the emergency services - five minutes before, to be precise,' said Tanya in a calm, controlled voice.

'I - I don't remember,' was the hesitant reply.

'We have another problem we can't get to grips with, Mrs Watts,' said the DI. 'We haven't found the knife used in the attack. No sign of it.'

'But we did find traces of blood, Mrs Watts, in your lounge and kitchen. The thing is, no matter how many times you try to clean it, traces always remain,' chipped in Tanya.

'Oh dear,' was the only response from "Dusty". She glanced at her solicitor, leant across and whispered in his ear.

Mr Brocklebank stopped chewing the end of his pen and leant forward, resting his elbows on the table. 'Officers, Mrs Watts would like to make a statement.' "Dusty" took another tissue from her bag, dabbed her nose, screwed the tissue into a ball and held it tight in her clenched hands.

Dave stood up, went to the door and asked the constable to bring some fresh tea and coffee. 'Biscuits, Mrs Watts?' Mrs Watts nodded her head and mumbled her thanks through the soggy tissue she held close to her mouth and nose. Brocklebank whispered into his client's ear and she

182

nodded repeatedly in answer. Both sat upright when the constable knocked at the door and entered with the refreshments.

DI Gowan looked across to Tanya. 'When you're ready, Mrs Watts.' He looked up at the wall clock. It was 4:30 p.m. 'In your own words, tell us what happened.'

'Like I said the first time, I came home from work at the usual time. Me 'usband 'ad already gone to work. I put the key in the lock and opened the front door. I don't know why, but it didn't feel right. Anyway, I just stood there for a minute, then I 'eard 'im, I could 'ear the bugger upstairs.' Sipping her tea, she looked from one officer to the other. 'I didn't know what to do, so I crept into the living room, I could still hear him moving about upstairs. I got me mobile out of me bag and called Steve. 'E told me stay where I was and not to do owt. I went into the kitchen and took a knife off the draining board, went back into the living room and just stood there. Next thing I knew, I 'eard Steve shouting from the front door, then there was a pounding on the stairs as 'e ran down and pushed Steve out of the way. When 'e came into the living room, 'e just ran into me. I was 'olding me arm straight out, pointing the knife, and 'e just ran straight onto it. I couldn't believe it. It went right in. Next thing, 'e pushed me away and managed to run out the back door.'

The tissue was in shreds as Mrs Watts picked at it with her pudgy fingers, then screwed the bits together and wiped her nose. 'I ran outside after 'im and 'e bumped into them lads. I ran back in and told Steve and 'e said we will be alright, we could blame the lads. Steve 'ad already started to

183

clean the blood off the carpet with some stuff I got from work and I rang 999.'

It was nearly an hour later when Mrs Watts was led away to the cells by a uniformed officer.

Chapter 20

The snow had been steadily falling all day, causing traffic chaos throughout the city. By the evening rush hour there were traffic jams on all the major routes. The buses were running late and trains had been cancelled. Many city commuters decided to leave their vehicles and opt for the unreliable public transport, however hit and miss it might be.

Marlowe took a look out of his office window. The day shift were getting ready for the off, working hard with their scrapers, clearing away the day's snow before heading home. Marlowe decided to hang on at the station a little later than usual to give the traffic a chance to ease off but, in reality, it didn't make a lot of difference. The drive home to Beverley that evening was horrendous. The traffic tailed back for miles, even though the snow had eased off slightly. What was usually a journey of around forty minutes took an hour and a half to travel the eight miles up the A1174.

The snow lay deep along the towpath and Marlowe had to negotiate the Mondeo with extra care along the side of the Beck. He fastened up his wax jacket, pulled his woollen City hat down over his ears and got out of the car. He struggled to pull the compound gates open across the snow, which had lain there drifting all day. Scraping, pulling and kicking, he eventually managed to get the gates open wide enough to drive through. He wished he had just left the car on the towpath.

He could see the light on in Joyce and Harry's cottage. Footsteps led from the cottage to the Daisy, one set human and the other canine. It looked as if Archie had spent another day with his adopted friends.

The warmth hit him as he stepped down into the galley, Harry had been stocking up the solid fuel boiler and a welcoming casserole prepared by Joyce was on the unit, waiting to be heated up. Marlowe followed his regular routine of feeding and watering Archie first, then put his dinner on a slow heat and headed for the shower. Feeling refreshed, and dressed in jogging bottoms and a sweatshirt, he headed for the galley and opened a bottle of Shiraz. After a hot meal and a glass or two of vino, he was asleep in minutes.

* * *

Preparation was everything; you got that right and nothing could go wrong. He'd been taught this as a young man learning his trade. He looked like the abominable snowman as he waited for a bus. He didn't want to risk a taxi. To be on the safe side, he got off the bus two stops before he needed to. It paid to be cautious. It was only a ten minute walk from the bus stop to the lock-up. There was a fair amount of traffic moving steadily through the thick wet slush and snow. He kept his head down and walked, avoiding eye contact with the other insane people walking the streets.

The van started first time, filling the lock-up with fumes. He opened the door, went back outside, and started scraping the snow away from the double doors.

The snow melted on his shaved head and dripped down his neck. He ran his hands across the stubble. Once the job was done, he went back inside and slid open the bolts. Heaving with his shoulders, he pushed the doors open wide and backed the van out of the workshop. He left the engine running and went back inside. It was freezing. His breath came out of his mouth like steam from a condenser. The man brought his cupped hands to his mouth and blew, then rubbed them together before he checked the contents of his tool bag. Everything was ok. He looked around him; everything was in place - the plastic, the chair and the tools he had placed on the workbench.

He lifted the corner of the dirty sacking covering the window. It was all clear. He turned off the light before opening the snicket door and closed it behind him. He put the padlock in place and snapped the lock shut. He walked around the van, opened the driver's side door and kicked the snow off his feet as he climbed in. Turning the ignition key, he set the heater to maximum.

It was time.

Regardless of the snow, the traffic was heavier than he'd expected. The Clive Sullivan Way was tailing back from the other side of the city centre. There was no alternative but to sit in the line of vehicles, and wait.

* * *

As soon as DI Gowan had seen the weather that morning, he decided to bite the bullet and go and see Joan and the kids for an hour after work, regardless of what the old bag would say. Half an hour in the snow and a bit of fun with the kids was all he asked. It wasn't too much.

It obviously was.

'Sorry,' she'd told him, 'I've got something organised.'

Same old story. He'd just about begged, it did no good. He put it all down to the dragon lady.

His next option was the obvious one - go out and get pissed out of his mind - but he reluctantly decided on the sensible option, a takeaway and a couple of bottles of Bud whilst watching Hull City's night match away against Ipswich on Sky television.

Gowan pulled the car onto the forecourt outside his Victorian three-bedroomed terraced home down Alliance Avenue. The concrete forecourt was once the front garden. He'd had it converted when Joan was still living there to make parking easier.

Gowan nudged the car as far as he could to the front wall of the house and turned off the engine. He wrapped a woolly scarf around his neck and stepped into the snow. Pulling his coat collar up, and with his hands tucked deep in his pockets, he set off on foot to the Golden Dragon takeaway.

The steam came out of the building like a fog as he opened the door and went inside, shutting the snow out behind him. The takeaway was empty. Not surprising on a night like this, he thought. The DI did a quick scan of the menu fixed high above the counter and settled for a prawn curry with rice.

Back in the house, with his shoes off and his slippers on, he managed to balance the takeaway on his knees. Two empty bottles of Bud were on the coffee table in front of him. 'Go on,' he shouted at the television, almost spitting out a mouthful of rice over the screen as City ploughed into the Ipswich goal area. 'Yes,' he shouted as City went one-nil in front. He'd shovelled in another mouthful of curry just as his mobile rang. 'Gowan,' he answered incoherently.

'Dave, it's Pat in the control room.' Pat Johnson was the duty inspector in the central control room. Pat and Dave Gowan had joined the force at the same time and they had both done their probationary period at Hull's Tower Grange Station in the east of the city and remained good friends ever since. 'I know you're off duty, but I thought you would want to know, looks like we may have had a hit on the mystery van with the CCTV.'

Gowan put down his plate. 'Whereabouts?' he asked as he turned down the volume on the television.

'Just coming up to the city centre slip road, near the Garrison Way roundabout, about five minutes ago.'

'Are you sure it's him?' asked the DI.

'Not hundred percent but it looks good. There was a Road Traffic Collision at the Myton Street junction and all the traffic was diverted. Only picked it up because things were at a standstill.'

'Let's not get too excited yet. Can you divert a couple of extra cars in the town to see if they can spot him? Check further back on the CCTV and see if you can find out where he came on.'

'No problem.'

'I'll wait for you to get back to me before I call the PI. No point in dragging him back from Beverley until we've got something more positive.'

Gowan pressed the button and ended the call. He picked up his bottle of Bud and brought it up to his lips, then thought better of it. He returned it to the table, picked up his mobile again and dialled. 'Phil, it's Dave,' he said into the handset and repeated the conversation he'd just had.

'You did right. No point being too ambitious at the moment. Give Jenny and the team a call. Put them on standby. As soon as you hear anything more, let me know. If we're lucky, you'd better get them to send a traffic car for me. Snow's pretty bad near here.' Not to mention that he'd had two or more glasses of red. Marlowe walked through to the galley and poured himself another glass of Shiraz. He had a good feeling about this. With luck this could be the break they'd been waiting for.

'Looks like I could be going out, Archie,' he told the dog laid out on the dinette seat like he owned it. He took his drink back through to the lounge and sat next to the dog, waiting for the call.

* * *

He knew the snow wouldn't stop the dealer from going to the Sailor if he could make a quid or two. The journey took longer than he'd expected. He'd had to run the van blower on full to keep the windscreen clear of condensation as he sat in the tail-back of vehicles. As he drew closer to the town, he could see the hold-up was caused by drivers rubbernecking at an accident between a bus and a

190

motorcycle on the slip road. The motorcycle was sticking out from under the bus. In the distance he could hear a siren approaching. Officers on the scene in hi-visibility jackets urged him on as he crawled past the accident.

He was almost positive he wouldn't be recognised with his cropped hair; nevertheless, he kept his head tilted down as the traffic moved. He'd no option but to carry on at a snail's pace to the next exit. He turned off at the Garrison Way roundabout and headed back towards the old town over the Drypool Bridge. The tide was out and he could see even the murky mud flats of the river were starting to become whited over as the snow continued to fall.

As he came into the city area, he was surprised at how many people there were about, mostly young people. Then again, it was a Friday night. It took a lot more than a bit of bad weather to stop the youngsters from enjoying themselves. He thought how ridiculous they looked standing outside the pubs smoking and shivering, especially the girls wearing their low hung jeans and flimsy tops, their bare midriffs exposed to the elements. He turned the van right and felt the skin prickle at the back of his neck as the back end of the van slipped when he crossed the snow-rutted junction. Still moving at a snail's pace, he drove down the narrow road past the old Salvation Army building and made for the same vantage point he'd used the last time he'd visited the Sailor.

* * *

Marlowe sat in the Daisy's saloon trying to relax with his evening paper, the Hull Daily Mail, and another glass of Shiraz, but he was finding it difficult to turn off. Even the

191

wine wasn't helping. He laid the newspaper down in front of him and glanced up at the television fixed high on the bulkhead opposite. The BBC News was about to start. He picked up the remote control and increased the volume.

There was the usual stuff about the economic crisis and the Government reform of the Social Security system and the new pension plans. Thankfully, there was only a brief mention of his case on the national news. He was relieved that there wasn't a hyped-up story on the murders.

Marlowe picked up his glass and sipped the wine while he watched the misery that was going on around the world. This made him feel even more disheartened. He continued watching, expecting more in-depth coverage of the murders on the local news that followed the main bulletin.

Finally, he couldn't wait for Dave any longer, picked up his mobile and dialled. 'Dave, it's Phil. Heard anything yet?'

'Not so far. Pat's still getting the CCTV checked out and we've put extra area cars in the vicinity. What with the weather conditions, I'm not holding my breath.' Gowan was watching the television as he spoke. Ipswich had equalised and he had to stop himself from swearing aloud down the phone.

'Ok, keep me posted.'

Marlowe reached out for the wine bottle and stopped. A cup of coffee might be more sensible, he thought, and went through to the galley, with Archie close on his heels, hoping for a trip up on the deck. When he returned to the saloon the news report on Look North was starting. With his mug of coffee in his hands, he sat waiting. Marlowe watched the presenter, Gordon Clarke, report in detail on the weather and the associated disruption it was causing throughout the city and surrounding areas. What came next wasn't what he had anticipated. The presenter turned his head sideways and picked up another camera for dramatic effect. He paused slightly and stared directly into the lens. "Earlier today, police confirmed that the body of the man found in the Wiltshire Road area of Hull was that of a twenty six year old man living locally, James Wood. Mr Wood is said to be originally from Leeds and has been living in Hull for the past eighteen months. Sources revealed Mr Wood was known to have been involved in the local drugs scene. Circumstances surrounding his death are still somewhat of a mystery. His body was found in the early hours of yesterday morning, wrapped in polythene sheeting. It has been revealed the victim suffered a serious and brutal head injury. At this stage, police are neither confirming nor denying whether the incident is connected to the death of another known drug dealer, Thomas Gleeson, whose body was found under similar circumstances."

'Jesus,' Marlowe said aloud to the television screen, 'the public will think we have a bloody serial killer on the loose.'

* * *

The blower was on full power, keeping the condensation at bay. The van had skidded several times and the snow was still coming down at a fair rate. He struggled to see between the slapping of the wiper blades and swore at the weather. He was beginning to think perhaps he should have given it a miss. The white stuff was starting to build up in layers on the screen at either side of the wipers. To say the very least, visibility was now really crap. *Big mistake*, he thought to himself. Even if he was in the pub, it would look too fucking obvious. The place would probably be nigh-on empty.

Slowly and carefully, he brought the van to a sliding stop just after the Cannon Street corner and sighed. For a couple of minutes he just sat there, staring through the steaming up windscreen. *Bastard.* With the decision made, he turned off the wipers but left the van engine running. He stepped down from the van into the deep freezing white crystals and kicked his way to the front of the vehicle. With a gloved hand, he did his best to clear the compacting snow off the windscreen. It was solid and the job took longer than he thought it would. When the screen was reasonably clear, he climbed back in and fastened his seat belt. Once composed. He slipped the gear lever into reverse and eased the Transit around the corner, making deep tyre tracks in the virgin snow. Already the snow was filling the tracks he had made. What option did he have? There was fuck all he could do about it. The buses had stopped running and taxis were like rocking horse shit. Walking wasn't an option; neither was leaving the van.

Chapter 21

Marlowe had another restless night. He woke up again on the dinette, his body aching as he struggled to get to his feet. The television was still turned on.

He hobbled his way through to the galley, filled the kettle, turned it on and headed for a quick shower while it boiled. Feeling slightly better after his shower, he threw a tea bag into a mug and filled it with boiling water. He then let Archie up on deck in the snow for his constitutional. Clambering back down below deck to the galley, and still feeling the effects of too much alcohol, he settled for his mug of builder's tea.

The snow lay thick in the compound and he decided to leave Archie on board the Daisy. He knew it wouldn't be too long before Harry came to collect him.

As the DCI drove into the station car park, he couldn't help but notice someone had been busy. The snow had been cleared and piled up against the walls, and rock salt had been spread everywhere. *Bet your bottom dollar it won't have been Cleevsey*, he thought to himself.

'Morning, Maigret. What was the drive in like?' asked Cleeves as the DCI stepped through the custody door from the parking area.

'Not half as bad as I was expecting, Trev. Once I'd managed to get the car out of the compound, and then diced with death along the towpath without driving into the Beck, it was ok. Main roads aren't too bad. It said on radio the snow ploughs and gritters had been out all night.'

Cleeves lay across the high desk, resting on his elbows, and looked down to the floor. 'I was half expecting to see Archie pulling you in on a sledge,' chuckled the sergeant.

'Yeah, yeah, yeah,' Marlowe smiled.

'You'd better have these.' Cleeves handed across a file containing the overnight crime reports.

The DCI took the thin manila folder from the sergeant. 'Looks good, Trev,' he said as he flipped through the documents. 'True to form, the bad weather usually keeps the buggers in front of the telly. At least that's one thing we can always count on.'

Coronation Street, *Emmerdale* and the *Bill*, the usual topics of early morning conversations in the squad room, had been replaced with snow, snow and more snow. Who had almost been snowed in, whose journey was the most hazardous, and so the conversations went on for a while longer until the office door opened and slammed shut again.

'Morning, all. Glad to see you've all made it in.'

'Can't let a bit of snow get in the way, Boss. Is there much out your way?' asked Lee with a broad grin on his face while he focused on his computer screen.

'Enough,' Marlowe stopped him short, determined to avoid getting into a snowy conversation. 'When you've got a minute, Dave, we need to do a catch up, and bring a coffee with you.'

The DI shook his head. 'He's got a bloody coffee machine and yet I always get caught for it,' he mumbled to no one in particular as he went out to the vending machine in the corridor.

* * *

There had been no further snowfalls. Public transport was running more or less on time, apart from one or two delays to inbound trains, but on the whole, things were starting to look up. The council had been ploughing and gritting the city thoroughfares all night, trying to keep disruption to a minimum.

Hull Kingston Rovers, one of the local rugby league teams, had a home match in the evening and the ground staff had started to clear the pitch and the car park at first light.

'I've already told you to stop messing about. There's a lot to do,' the Hull K.R. steward shouted across the car park to the young man who was throwing snowballs instead of clearing the snow away.

'Oh, come on, Bill, it's only a lark. Here, cop this.' Laughing, he stretched back his arm and threw a hard ball of frozen snow and ice at his mate.

The steward saw the snowball coming, but there was little he could do to avoid the frozen lump. 'You little sod!'

Shouting, he dodged to the left and, caught off-guard, he slipped on the compacted snow. His feet lost contact with the ground and he went arse over tit into a drift against the fence.

'You stupid bugger I could have broke me friggin' neck,' he yelled back.

He tried to push himself up and his left arm disappeared into the deep drift and stopped just below the surface. He pushed himself around and rested on his side. 'Fucking Hell, give me your mobile.'

* * *

'Cheers, Dave,' said Marlowe from behind his desk as he reached across for the plastic cup Dave was offering him. 'I take it Pat got no further with the CCTV last night?'

'Not a cat in hell's chance,' Dave answered as he sat down on the vacant chair. 'I don't like to keep harping on about it, but it was the bloody snow - just about wiped out all the CCTV vision. You couldn't see a thing on the Clive Sully cameras. The snow was blowing straight off the river.' He took a sip of his coffee and carried on. 'The only reason we got an ID on the van earlier was because traffic was stationary due to the RTC between a bus and a motorcycle.'

'Never had one of them. You?'

'Had what?'

'Motorbike. Have you ever had one?'

'No chance. Like my comforts too much.'

Jenny sat at her desk, leaning forward on her elbows, resting her chin on her cupped hands, when the telephone rang and startled her out of her train of thought.

'CID, Detective Sergeant Bright,' Jenny said into the telephone handset as she brought it up to her ear. She covered the handset with the palm of her hand. 'Our counterparts at Tower Grange,' she mouthed to Tanya.

'Hang on, yes, thanks, it's just arrived,' Jenny said as her computer announced the arrival of an email. 'Thanks very much, sir. I'll be in touch shortly.'

The DS pressed the print button on her keyboard and walked across to the laser printer to retrieve the message. She shook her head as she stood and read the report.

Marlowe and Gowan looked towards the door as Jenny knocked and walked in, waving the email.

'Yes, Jenny, what can I do for you?' asked Marlowe as she closed the door behind her.

'I've just had a call from control at Tower Grange. One of their inspectors just sent this. You'd better have a read, Boss.'

The DCI adjusted his spectacles and sat back to read the email.

'Oh, for fuck's sake, this is all we need,' Marlowe growled as he passed the piece of paper over to the DI. 'That explains last night. No fucking wonder he never showed up anywhere in the city centre again. He was off to watch the friggin' rugby.'

Within five minutes of the steward's call to the emergency services, the Hull Kingston Rovers car park was surrounded by blue flashing lights and blue and white plastic incident tape. Almost as soon as Marlowe finished reading the email, he was up on his feet and half way through the door with his coat in his hand. 'Well, what are you waiting for? Get your coats.'

Dave jumped up from his chair and nearly tripped over Jenny as they both tried to get through the door at the same time.

Marlowe was already in the Mondeo with the engine running, tapping his hands impatiently on the steering wheel, when they appeared less than two minutes later. The DI flew around to the front passenger side and almost dived into the car. As soon as Jenny slammed the back door shut, the DCI was pulling out into Gordon Street. With the blue flashing light stuck to the roof of the Mondeo, and a "wannabe" Formula One driver behind the wheel, they made good progress as Marlowe weaved in and out of the traffic.

Marlowe was on tenterhooks; this could provide them with the lead they were looking for.

There was no mistaking the murder site. The blue flashing lights could be seen from half way down Holderness Road. The DCI pulled the Ford Mondeo up as close as he could to the cordoned-off area, just behind the ambulance already on the scene. 'Who's in charge here?' he shouted from the open car door.

'That would be me, sir,' answered a voice with a distinct Scottish accent. The voice belonged to the DS from the Tower Grange Police station. The DS himself looked as if he could be a rugby league player, tall with broad shoulders, with his neck almost disappearing into his body. Marlowe recognised the voice immediately and turned to face its owner, Detective Sergeant Callum McCraig.

'Well I never. I thought you were still north of the border,' Marlowe said with a touch of surprise in his voice.

The DCI walked around to the boot of the car and popped the lid. He fished about and took out his emergency forensic kit of disposable overalls and over-shoes.

Dave Gowan and Jenny did the same, struggling to keep their feet on the icy surface of the car park as they put on their white paper suits.

'Well, you know what it's like, sir. Can't keep a good dog down. Besides, it's a bloody sight warmer down 'ere.' His Scottish accent had more than a trace of 'ull as he dropped his "h's" and flattened his vowels.

Marlowe was still struggling with his paper suit, looking as if he was putting on a straitjacket.

'How long have you been back?' he asked as he laboured with his hands around his back, trying to reach the armholes.

'About three months, give or take.'

'Did you bring Marie back with you?'

'Aye, well, that's a story for another day, preferably over a pint.'

Marlowe just raised his eyebrows at the answer and got the message. 'Ok, Callum, let see what we've got.'

'Right you are, sir. Over there by the fence.'

'How long have you been on the scene?'

'Just nicely arrived before yourselves.'

DCI Marlowe and his team followed McCraig across the car park. Marlowe didn't give them much of a chance to clear away the snow before the match with Leeds Rhinos. As per usual, the immediate vicinity had been cordoned off with even more of the blue and white tape.

'Who found the body?' the DCI asked as he looked around, his eyes taking it all in. He thought it strange for a killer to dump the body so near to the entrance. *Why here and not off the beaten track?* He thought.

'Ground staff - two lads trying to clear the car park for tonight's match. They were arsing about and the steward fell and landed on the body. I've got someone taking their statements as we speak.'

'Let's hope he hasn't contaminated any evidence. We're not having much success with this case so far. To be honest, we've still got bugger-all to go on. This could be the break we've been waiting for.' Marlowe shook his head, 'For fuck's sake, I wish I wouldn't keep saying that.'

'What's happening with SOCO?' asked DI Gowan over the DCI's shoulder as they trudged along behind. The well-worn path was turning into a mucky slush. Jenny thought it quite comical. All dressed in their white paper suits as they made their way across the car park; she thought they looked like a bunch of snowmen going to a convention.

'Should be with us any time now, Dave,' answered McCraig. 'Apparently they got held up behind an articulated lorry that jack knifed across Drypool Bridge.'

The site was a mass of activity. The heavy police presence and flashing lights had attracted quite a few spectators to the murder scene. No sooner had the uniformed officers at the car park entrance cleared them away than another nosey bunch took their place.

'Morning, sir,' said a young uniformed constable securing the immediate area. Marlowe nodded. The constable lifted the plastic incident tape to allow Marlowe get a better view of the macabre snowy mound.

'Sure no one else has been near the body?' he asked as he took a pair of latex gloves out of his pocket and put them on.

'No, sir. Only the constable first on the scene.'

'Not you, then?'

'No, sir.' The PC nodded towards his colleague on the perimeter.

'Right, then, let's take advantage of no SOCO and take a look.'

Marlowe carefully checked the snow around the body so as not to disturb any evidence that might be lurking below. When he was sure he wouldn't contaminate the scene, he crouched down low. His knees creaked and his back twinged as he got lower - too many nights on the dinette. With the fingers of his gloved hand, he carefully brushed the snow off the polythene sheeting, just enough until he could see the face clearly that lay below the white flaky surface.

Through the plastic sheeting, the DCI could see a small round open mouth with bright red, pursed lips and fixed staring bright blue eyes, shrouded in stringy blonde hair.

'Callum, you'd better take a look at this.' DS McCraig looked at Dave and Jenny, then back to Dave, before hesitantly making his way forward. Marlowe still had his back to the team as DS McCraig edged under the tape and crouched down beside him. 'Well?' said Marlowe. 'What do you make of that?' Smiling, he turned his head towards the DS, watching his response.

Callum couldn't believe his eyes. A full murder team on site, blue flashing lights everywhere, a team of paramedics and SOCO on the way, all because some arsehole thought it would be funny to bury... 'A BLOW UP FUCKING DOLL,' he shouted.

On hearing this, Jenny and Dave looked at one another and found it impossible not to laugh loudly at the outburst.

'Alright you two, that's enough. Save it for the pub,' said the DCI, looking over his shoulder, still smiling. Marlowe and McCraig stood up and looked down at the body, 'What do you reckon, Callum. She's not too bad looking. A bit rubbery, mind you. Fancy your chances? I don't reckon she'd put up much resistance?'

'Piss off, sir,' DS McCraig replied, knowing the DCI wouldn't take offence. 'What a fuck-up. Better call the lads off. I'll let SOCO have a look, though. They might be able to throw some light on whoever the joker is.'

'Right, then, Callum, we'll be off and leave you to it,' Marlowe called over his shoulder as he walked back.

Dave turned to Jenny and gave her a wink. 'Don't forget,' he called over his shoulder as they trudged back up the snowy path, 'if you need any help, or if she goes down and you need a bicycle pump, just give one of us a call.' They were still laughing when they reached the car.

The drive back to the Gordon Street nick was at a more sedate speed compared to their outward journey, complete with a number of pervy jokes, all at Callum's expense.

'I wouldn't be surprised if Callum isn't back over the border guarding haggis by the time his shift's over.'

Gowan couldn't help but laugh at his own joke. Jenny and Marlowe just shook their heads.

Chapter 22

Another day nearly over, and still they didn't have any significant leads. *Two dead bodies and a blow up doll, what a mess*, the DCI thought to himself.

Marlowe eased back in his chair and stretched out his legs. His calves felt tight, as if he might get cramp. He took off his spectacles and dropped them down on the desk. With the back of his hands, he rubbed his gritty eyes as he yawned. He put his spectacles back on and tidied his desk ready for a new day.

'That's me done,' he called out into the main office. He could see that everyone was winding down. The late shift was already making an appearance.

'Not coming for a pint, sir?' asked Jenny.

'No thanks, Jenny. I've had enough for one day.' He'd let them go and have a laugh at Callum's expense; they'd already had one at his.

'Are you coming, Lee?'

'You must be kidding, I've got better things to do than sit in the George with you lot.' He stood up from his desk, stretched and reached for his jacket.

'What's more important than going for a pint with your mates?' asked the DI.

'Got a date - need I say more?'

Gowan smiled and shook his head. 'Jonno, are you up for a session?'

'Well, as much as I'd like to, I don't think the missus will be very pleased if I let my tea get cold.'

'What a bloody shambles,' said the DI. 'Looks like it's just you and me, kid,' he said to Jenny.

'What makes you think I'm coming? Am I so predictable?' Jenny swung around on her chair.

Gowan grabbed his jacket. 'Just going to the loo before we go,' he announced, and disappeared.

'You're not going to leave me alone with the old crooner, are you, Tanya?' Jenny asked.

'Just give me five minutes and I'll catch you up.' With that, Tanya did an about-turn, switched off her computer and made a grab for her bag and coat. 'Hang on, this can wait 'till morning, I can only stop for one.'

'Don't worry about it. You can stop at mine if we have too many.'

By the time the team was leaving the nick, just about everything on the transport front was back to normal. The roads were clear, and the trains and buses were running to time. The weather had changed for the better. The wind had swung around towards the west, blowing the snow out over the North Sea. All along the north bank of the Humber Estuary, the snow had given way to a light drizzle and the winter wonderland was fast turning to mucky brown slush.

It was not so pleasant for the evening pedestrians. They trudged along the slushy pavements, dodging as the traffic sped past, spraying them with muck.

* * *

It had been a long day. It had been late by the time the Nail Man had driven back in the blizzard the previous evening. After a couple of stiff drinks sat in front of the gas fire, he thought it best to try and get some rest. He knew it would be a long time before sleep overtook him.

He poured himself another near-full tumbler of whisky and took it up the stairs with him. He set the glass down on the bedside cabinet and, fully clothed, lay back on the pillows, thinking. Why had it happened? It wasn't as if they'd been bad parents. When they knew the worst, he'd gone out to buy the drugs himself. It wasn't as if he didn't know where to get them.

But the day he'd come home early while his wife was still at work had been the last straw. No television, no DVD player and even the tumble drier and washing machine had gone. The bastard had sold the lot. *What else could he have done?* He wondered. There was no other option but to throw him out. His wife had reluctantly agreed; they had done all they could.

Tomorrow night, he decided. Tomorrow.

* * *

From his vantage point, tucked in the warehouse doorway, the only sound he could hear was that of the pigeons cooing and flapping through the broken windows as they competed for a roosting spot amongst the roof timbers. He'd stood there freezing his bollocks off for the past hour, watching the cars, vans and lorries go past.

A taxi pulled up. He was so cold now he could hardly feel his toes. Then it happened. This was it. A light coloured Ford Mondeo private hire car pulled up right outside the pub door. He saw Barnes get out of the back passenger seat and walk around to the driver's window. He passed something through the open window. *Probably paying the fare*, he thought. He could hear him saying something to the driver, unfortunately, he was too far away to make out what it was. Despite the cold, he decided to wait a little longer.

Pete Barnes walked straight through the pub and stood in the dingy car park with his hands cupped around his cigarette. In the shelter of the back porch, he took a deep drag of the smoke, threw the cigarette to the floor and crushed the butt with his heel into the slush before he went back inside.

Across the road, the man stamped his feet and blew onto his hands to keep the circulation going. Suddenly, on impulse, he walked straight across to the pub. The warmth greeted him as he pushed open the solid wooden door. He felt nervous. He shouldered his way through the crowd to the bar. The bottle-blonde serving behind it had her work cut out with the throng of customers but eventually he caught her eye.

'Yes, love, what can I get you?' she asked pleasantly.

'A pint of best, please.' He tried not to make eye contact as he fished around in his pocket, apprehensively looking around the busy bar at the same time. Then he saw him.

Blondie placed his drink on the bar towel in front of him and he paid. His hands were visibly shaking.

'Are you alright, love?' she asked. Without replying, he carelessly turned around almost too quickly and only just avoided spilling his pint over one of the darts players.

'Watch it, mate,' the big bloke behind him said aggressively as he juggled with a full glass.

'Sorry,' was all he could manage as he kept his head down, keeping Barnes in his vision. Not wanting a repeat performance, he made his way across to the noisy end of the bar, squeezing into a corner adjacent to the main door. He was sure he was out of Barnes' line of sight. At the same time, the position offered him the perfect place where he could keep an eye on his quarry.

He leant against the wall, sipping his pint and watching, trying not to look conspicuous. This wasn't a hard task, given his extreme appearance. He thought he looked like half of the weirdoes in this place.

Pete Barnes, minus his brother for company, looked his usual self - a wannabe. His brother Gary was away in Manchester for a couple of days, sorting out some merchandise. He should have been back last night, but Pete hadn't heard from him. He wasn't unduly worried; he'd done it before. Pete thought it more than likely he'd shacked up with some tart for the duration.

Barnes sat at his usual back corner table where he could keep an eye on who was coming through the pub door. It looked like he was deep in a whispered conversation with a "business associate". All the while, the man kept on sipping and watching as various dubious characters went across to have words with Barnes. Most times they returned to their tables, but on occasion they would both go out of the back door and two minutes later Barnes would return alone.

Two pints later he glanced at his watch; it was not far off last orders. *Soon be time*, he thought to himself. He could feel the adrenaline surging. His heart began to beat faster as if it was trying to escape through his chest wall. He put down his glass on the window sill and wiped his sweaty palms down the side of his trouser legs.

After taking a series of controlled breaths to steady himself, he walked across to the bar once more. He squeezed in sideways between the drinkers and almost had to shout to make himself heard as someone opened the door to the upstairs concert room. The music pounded all over the pub. 'Two pints of best, please, love,' he shouted over the music. The girl nodded. Glancing over his shoulder, he could see Barnes still sat at the table, alone.

'Five pounds forty, please, darlin'.' She passed across the drinks and put them down, as before, on the bar towel in front of him. He muttered his thanks and paid. This time he turned around carefully. With a pint in each hand, he took another deep breath and made his move. Steadily, he made his way through the punters, heading towards the table where his quarry sat. *Easy now*, he thought to himself, *let him make the first move, give him space, let him get confident.* He didn't speak or make a movement; he just stood there in front of the table with a pint in each hand and put one down in front of Barnes.

'What the fuck do you want?' Barnes said through gritted teeth. ''Ang on a minute, don't I know you?'

With the recognition, his attitude changed abruptly and he relaxed. *Too fucking right you do*, were Nail Man's thoughts. Keeping calm, he nodded.

'Got it. Tom, Dick, or was it Harry?' Barnes laughed at his own joke. 'Well, seeing as though you're bearing gifts, you might as well sit down.' Barnes kicked out his leg under the table and pushed out a chair.

Nail Man's nerves started to calm a little as he arranged the drinks on the grimy table top and pulled the chair all the way out. He sat down, still not saying anything.

'You nearly threw me there.' Barnes stared at the shaved head. 'It's that fucking haircut. It's crap.' He laughed again, picked up the drink and downed half of it in one go. 'Well, what is it?'

Time to speak. 'What's what?'

'Your name, you soft twat, what is it?'

'Does it matter?' *I know yours, you vulgar piece of shit*, he thought.

Barnes picked up his glass and swallowed down what was left. He wiped the back of his hand across his mouth. 'To be honest, I don't give a toss. Your round, I think.'

* * *

After a Marks and Spencer prepared meal of lasagne and fresh vegetables, cooked in the microwave and washed down with a couple of glasses of Piermont - a classic red from the Astir region of Italy, Marlowe started to relax too. The food, and especially the wine, were having the desired effect.

The frustrations of the case were getting the better of him. Two bodies, a blow up doll, and fuck-all to go on, so to speak. Decision made, he turned on the television with the volume down in the background and spread out the sports pages of the Hull Daily Mail across the dinette table. Right across the back page, the headline reads, "City Fiasco". *Not again*, he thought, as he studied the report. *Lost again, Ipswich 2, City 1.*

Mellow, that's how Marlowe thought he felt- not pissed, just mellow. He stood up, wavering slightly, and went through to the galley. He put on a pair of wellingtons and his thick coat and, armed with his cigarettes in one hand and Archie's lead in the other, he ushered Archie through the hatch, up onto the aft deck.

The snow on the Beck side still lay thick and deep in the owners' compound, Marlowe didn't fancy having to go chasing after the dog in the snow, so he bent down and clipped on the flexi-lead, which let the dog wander a bit further away. From the Daisy, he could see a shadowy figure ambling down the towpath towards him. It looked as if he was weaving from side to side a little too much. Marlowe took his lighter from his pocket, cupped his hands against the wind and lit a cigarette, then put the lighter back in his pocket. By now, the staggering man was almost alongside the boat.

'Now then, Harry, how are you doing? Cold enough for you?' Marlowe asked Archie's adopted minder.

'Not bad, Phil. Don't mind the cold. It's been worse,' replied Harry, who was wrapped up as if he'd just trekked from the North Pole.

'Haven't seen you for a couple of days. Thought the weather must be keeping you in.' Marlowe gave the flexi-lead a tug.

'Take a bit more snow than this, Phil, and, besides, who do you think walks that bloody dog of yours - the abominable snowman?'

Marlowe smiled. If it hadn't been for Harry and Joyce, he would have had to get rid of Archie a long time ago.

'How's Joyce? Still keeping you busy?'

'Need you ask? As fit as ever, always busy, and because she likes to be busy herself, she keeps finding me jobs to do. That's why I've sneaked out for a swift half, well a couple of pints, in the Sloop. Best get going. You know what she's like. Probably sat watching the clock as we speak. Night, Phil.'

'Good night, Harry. Take care.'

'Aye, see you tomorrow, son.'

Marlowe took a drag of his cigarette and started to wind Archie in.

'Right, Archie, time for bed.'

* * *

He picked up both empty glasses and went across to the bar for refills. When he came back, Barnes had disappeared. He hadn't seen his quarry leave. He didn't know if Barnes had gone for a piss or disappeared for the night.

Hoping for the best, he reached into his side jacket pocket and took out his handkerchief. Keeping his hands under the table, he very carefully shook a pill into the palm of his hand. There was still no sign of Barnes. He glanced around quickly without drawing attention to himself, and let his hand hover over Barnes' glass. He dropped the pill into the beer, swirled the glass around and pushed it across the table. His luck held. Barnes came swaggering back

213

across the bar like he owned it, distributing comments and slapping people on the back as he passed them.

'Just been for a piss,' he said as he sat down with his legs splayed out in front of him.

'Excuse me, love,' the blonde shouted across from behind the bar. He could feel his face colour up as he turned around to face her. 'You left your change.' He stood up and pushed back his chair, walked across and thanked the girl.

'Silly sod, what you blushing for? Fancy her, or sommat?'

He didn't reply, the small talk and snide remarks continued for the next ten minutes or so. By this time, he was starting to feel slightly pissed. He was only on his third pint. His eyes wouldn't focus and his speech was becoming slurred. He was finding it difficult to speak. Just the odd mumbled *fucking this and fucking that* came out of his mouth. He was making no sense at all and not even aware of it. The bass vibrating through the ceiling from the concert room didn't help his concentration. Something was wrong; it wasn't meant to be like this.

Barnes picked up his pint, took a long drink from it and drained the glass. He never took his eyes off the face opposite. By now his drinking partner was just about wrecked. He stood up from the table, pushed his chair back and walked around to the figure slouching in the chair opposite him. He stood behind him with his hands resting on his shoulders. The veins in the back of his hands stood out like lines on a map as he squeezed hard, yet the man in the chair was oblivious to pain. He just sat there mumbling to himself, not making any sense.

Barnes moved his hands under his armpits and made him rise to his feet, encountering no resistance. The chair scraped along the floor as the man stood with unsteady legs. He patted down the pockets. *Yes*, he thought to himself as he pulled out a set of car keys.

They both walked to the back door, one more capably than the other. Due to more luck than judgement, they managed to negotiate a path between the tables without causing too much havoc. 'Pissed,' Barnes said, rolling his eyes and shaking his head to people as they passed. No one gave them a second look.

Guiding him through the pub with a firm grip, he kicked open the back door. He felt his body waver as the fresh air hit him. 'Easy now,' he said as he used his free hand to point the key fob down the car park. The Transit's lights flickered as the doors unlocked. Both of them, hooked at the arm, skidded and slipped between the cars on the ice. He leaned him against the side of the van whilst he opened the passenger door. With a bit of pushing and goading, he managed to get him inside.

With some effort, he reached across and fastened him in with the seat belt. 'Clunk, click every trip,' he recited as he slammed the door shut. 'What a piece of shit you are. Fucking good job I switched drinks when you went back to the bar for your change. And there was me thinking you might have gobbed in mine.' Barnes spat the words out venomously into his companion's face and walked around the driver's side.

'Well, what the fuck am I gonna do with you now?' Barnes said to the comatose figure sat in the passenger seat.

215

He leaned across the seats and grabbed his face between both hands. Turning it towards him, he looked straight into the glassy eyes. 'Expect me to take you home and tuck you in? I don't fucking think so.'

* * *

The George was packed with weekend drinkers. Many of the younger locals would start off there with a couple of rounds before getting a taxi into the town. Two distinct groups dominated the bar area. There were the younger men in jeans and short sleeved shirts accompanying the girls with short tops and bare midriffs, the older men in their chinos and sweatshirts.

'I knew we shouldn't have come here tonight,' Jenny shouted across to Tanya as she fought her way back to the table with a tray of drinks. 'He's always the bloody same when there's karaoke on.'

An out-of-tune voice was giving an ear bashing rendition of Cat Stevens' *Moon Shadow*. The voice belonged to the DI.

'Do you think they know he's a copper?' Tanya asked when Jenny sat down.

'Most people must do, or they would have had him arrested by now for murdering a good song.' Jenny replied dryly as they watched Dave Gowan giving his excruciating performance on the small corner stage. His hair was all over the place. He'd taken off his tie and his face glistened with sweat under the spotlights. Swaying from side to side, he gestured with his left arm for the audience to join in, with the microphone in his right hand, nearly shoved half way down his throat.

'Keep watching.'

216

'Why? What am I watching for?'

'He's going to swallow that thing in a minute.'

Gowan took his bow to noisy applause and good humoured jeers, and went back to sit with the girls, wiping the sweat off his face with the back of his hand as he went.

'Well, what did you think?' he asked seriously.

'Don't give up the day job,' they both said simultaneously and laughed again.

'Is this why the PI never came?' Tanya shouted as the next punter went up on the stage.

'I wouldn't be at all surprised. When he does come, he usually only stops for one, then goes home to the dog,' Jenny answered.

'Don't call him that in front of the Boss,' Dave advised as he picked up his drink.

'Call who what?' Tanya asked with a puzzled look on her face.

'The DOG. The Boss gets stroppy and says *He's got a name, it's Archie*. He's pulled me up for saying it. Very protective.' Dave smiled as he held the pint glass to his mouth and took a deep swallow. 'Another one, anybody?'

'No thanks, we're off after this. Tanya's staying over at my place.'

'Interesting!' he said jokingly to the frowns on their faces. 'Don't suppose there's room for me, then.'

'You don't deserve it, but if you want the sofa, you're welcome to it.' Jenny reached around the back of her chair for her coat.

'Thanks for the offer, but I prefer a bed. Lend us your phone, Tanya, to call for a taxi. My battery's nearly flat.'

217

'Don't bother. We'll drop you off if you stop prattling about and hurry up.'

'Cheers for that, I'll take you up on it. Can we stop at the takeaway on the way?'

Gowan picked up his pint and finished it off.

Parked out of sight between two buildings in St. Anne Street with the engine still running, Police Constable Raines opened his paper parcel.

'Cleevsey will have our guts for garters if he finds out.'

'He'll never find out. Keep the windows open to let the smell out,' replied his partner, PC Allen, as they sat having a supper of haddock and chips out of newspaper.

'It'll stink of vinegar in here for ages.'

'Oh, just shut up and eat your chips. I'll have 'em if you don't want 'em.' Raines reached across.

'Keep your fucking hands off. I'm starving.' He shoved a handful of greasy chips into his mouth and wiped his fingers down the side of his trousers. He then reached forward and took a can of coke off the dashboard top and pulled back the tab. The drink sprayed everywhere.

'That's all we need,' grumbled Raines. 'What the fuck? Did you see that?' A dark coloured Transit van with no lights was passing their concealed parking spot.

'I was enjoying them.' Allen bundled his oily package into the foot well of the squad car. 'Let's go see.' He put the car into gear and edged out into Anne Street. They could see the van in front of them still driving with no lights.

'I'll do a PNC check on the number plate,' said PC Allen as he squinted out of the front windscreen.

'No need, I think we have hit the jackpot this time. It's the van the CID bods are looking for.' Raines glanced at his colleague in disbelief. 'I'm telling you mate, I'm fucking sure.'

'I'll call it in. Better drop back a bit.' Allen's Airwave radio came to life as he pressed the talk button. 'Alfa three-one to control.' He passed his message on. 'Whatever you do, don't fucking lose him.'

* * *

Barnes looked in the rear view mirror and couldn't help but see the patrol car.

'Oh shit,' he exclaimed when he realised he'd driven half way across the town centre without the van lights on. He flicked his finger out and *click*, the lights came on. 'No problemo,' he said to his vacant looking passenger when he saw the patrol car drop back.

* * *

Gowan came out of the Chinese takeaway with a big grin on his face, armed with a paper carrier bag of goodies. Tanya put her finger to her lips, motioning for the DI to be quiet as he opened the back door of the car. She nodded towards Jenny, speaking on her mobile.

'What's going on?' he asked, still smiling like a prat.

Jenny clicked off her mobile. 'You can take that smirk off your face. We're going back to work.'

'Oh, for Christ's sake, I just want some food and my bed. What's happened now?' moaned the DI from the back of the car.

He lay back and yawned with his mouth so wide it looked as if it would split.

219

Barnes could still see the patrol car in the rear view mirror. It seemed to be keeping its distance since he'd switched the van lights on. He couldn't decide if they had just dropped back or they were tailing him. 'I told you there was no problem,' he said to the figure beside him.

He put his foot down on the accelerator pedal and the Transit jumped forward. This time he killed the lights intentionally and took a sharp left turn onto Silver Street and then another left. About twenty metres into the street, he pulled the van into the kerb side, still with the lights off. He kept watching the mirror mounted on the driver's side door and couldn't believe his luck. There was no sign of the patrol car.

'Piece of piss,' Barnes told his uncomprehending passenger, although he might as well have been talking to himself for all the response he was receiving. 'Just you sit there and relax. Enjoy the ride. We're nearly there now.'

* * *

Even though there had been no fresh snow fall all day, the roads around St. Anne Street were still treacherous. The snow that remained had become packed solid on the cobbled surface. PCs Raines and Allen kept their distance from the van in front, careful not to spook the driver. They watched as the van suddenly put a spurt on and disappeared around the tight curve in the road.

'Here we go,' said Raines as he jabbed his foot down harder on the accelerator. The patrol car reacted swiftly. Once around the bend and on the straight again, Raines slammed on the brakes. The car came to a sliding stop.

220

'Where the fuck is he?' Raines peered through the windscreen.

'Fucked if I know. I never even saw him turn off.'

'Oh, for Christ's sake, they'll fucking kill us.'

'Whoa there, who's driving?' Allen held his hands up in mock despair. 'Not me, that's for certain.'

'Cheers, and fuck you too. I'll double back. Keep your fucking eyes open or we'll both be for the high jump.' Raines could feel the perspiration start to run down the back of his neck. 'You'd better call it in.'

* * *

The harsh fluorescent lights gave a clinical atmosphere to the communications room at the Gordon Street nick. The bank of CCTV screens was manned by four PCSOs with earphones and microphones fixed over their heads as they sat at their stations, concentrating on the tasks before them. Each officer was responsible for four monitors whose screens were further sub-divided into eight sections of the city.

Jenny and Tanya, nursing mugs of coffee, stood talking over the evening's events with the uniformed sergeant unfortunate enough to be on duty. The corner table at the back of the communications room was cluttered with tin foil takeaway containers. DI Gowan sat amongst the debris, ploughing his way through egg fried rice and crispy duck. He was already onto his second pot of coffee when Marlowe came in.

The DCI looked tired. He was casually dressed in jeans and a sweatshirt.

'How's it going?' he asked as he draped his wax jacket over a vacant chair.

The news wasn't good. Jenny reluctantly turned to face the DCI. 'We've got a situation. They've lost him.' DS Bright tensed herself, waiting for the DCI to explode. The explosion never came. Marlowe kept extraordinarily calm. Gowan was gobsmacked when the expected outburst didn't materialise.

Marlowe picked up his jacket off the chair, turned his back on the officers and simply walked to the exit.

'I'll be in my office,' he said as he shut the door behind him. 'FUCKING WANKERS,' he yelled at the top of his voice when he was out in the corridor. 'WHAT A SET OF USELESS TOSSERS,' they heard him add as he stormed off.

'That went well,' the DI said, still sitting at the table while everyone else had their eyes fixed on the CCTV monitors.

Back in his office, Marlowe hung his jacket on the chrome stand, walked around the back of his desk and slumped down in his leather chair. He took off his spectacles and placed them on the desk. He leaned forward, pulled out the top drawer of his desk, lay back in his chair and rested his feet on the drawer. He closed his eyes. It was going to be a long night, he thought to himself.

* * *

Close to the river front, beneath the silhouette of the River Humber tidal barrier, Barnes drove the van onto a patch of waste ground. With the lights turned off, the van was barely visible and well out of sight of prying eyes. The man strapped in the passenger seat was still lolling. Scarcely twenty minutes had passed since they had left the pub.

Barnes unfastened his seat belt and had a rummage around in the front glove box of the van, looking for any information that would give him a clue as to the man's identity. There was nothing that would help - till receipts for fuel, an empty crisp packet, a chocolate biscuit wrapper, and just a few scraps of paper and a half-empty bottle of mineral water wedged between the top of the dashboard and the windscreen.

'You don't give much away, do you?' Barnes said as he started to go through the man's jacket pockets. 'Well, well, well, this is a surprise,' he declared as he emptied his wallet. 'You are a dark horse. I wouldn't have guessed it.' He studied the contents of the wallet carefully before putting them in his own pocket. He took the bottle of water off the dashboard, unscrewed the top and sniffed the contents to make sure it was only water. He took a deep swallow and put the bottle back where he found it.

Then he had an idea.

He took his mobile phone out of his pocket and dialled. 'It's me. Yeah, right. Listen, where are you? Never mind. I want you to pick me up. When? Now, you dickhead, that's why I'm calling,' he told the dickhead at the other end where he was and hung up. Reaching into the inside pocket of his jacket, he took out a small sealed clear plastic bag of brown powder. 'Nah, I won't be greedy.' He put his hand back in the pocket and grabbed the remaining four packets. 'Here we go.' He grabbed the man by the chin and pushed back his head, opening the man's mouth without any

223

trouble, and one-by-one he tipped the contents of the bags into the man's mouth. Next, he grabbed the water bottle off the dashboard and tipped its contents down his throat. With his hand placed under the chin, he held the mouth closed while his victim coughed and gagged as he was forced to swallow the drink. Barnes stopped. When the man had finished choking, he once again forced the bottle between his lips until it was empty.

With no memories and no struggles, Nail Man's fight with his demons was over. Not the way he would have wanted them to disappear, nevertheless it was over. He lost consciousness and drifted into a drug-induced coma.

Barnes sat back in the driving seat and sighed. He reached into the top zip pocket of his jacket and pulled out a wrap of his own personal stuff. He shook the white powder onto the dashboard and cut the powder into two lines with the plastic card he had just acquired. He rolled a ten pound note into a tube, brought it up to his nose and sniffed up the lines. *Magic*, he thought. Feeling relaxed and confident, he took the keys from the ignition and climbed out of the van, pressing the remote to lock the vehicle. Careful where he walked, he crossed the snowy waste ground until he reached the low brick wall. With the keys in his right hand, he drew back his arm in a wide swing and tossed them into the river as far as he could throw them.

He didn't look back at the van as he walked to where his lift should be waiting for him. He was smiling.

Chapter 23

The night was heading towards dawn as Raines and Allen continued their search for the missing vehicle. Out of a sense of guilt, they'd worked beyond the end of their shift finishing time.

'I'm knackered,' Raines grumbled. 'My eyes feel like piss holes in the snow.' He rubbed them with the backs of his hands.

'One last sweep. Head down High Street towards the river.' PC Allen was as tired as his mate. Raines turned the patrol car down the cobbled surface of the High Street in Hull's historic museum area. They passed the Street Life Museum on the left and the Old Black Boy public house. The night had remained snow free and, due to the lack of traffic in the area, combined with an overnight frost, the cobbled road was like glass. Allen and Raines crawled along. At each turn off and entrance that could conceal a vehicle, one of them left the patrol car armed with a powerful torch and conducted a thorough search. The painstaking procedure paid off. On waste ground near the Argos Super Store, they could see the silhouette of a Transit van glistening in their headlights. They'd found it.

* * *

Marlowe had been dozing on and off all night between frequent visits to the toilet and the communications room. DI Gowan had kept him company; not that he had been much company as he lay doubled up on the small sofa, open-mouthed and snoring.

The DCI stood with his back to the window, warming his rear end on the radiator.

'You know, Dave, I just can't comprehend how that pair of wankers lost them. Eleven o'clock at night, quiet road and no traffic!' he said as he stretched his arms above his head, trying to ease the knotted muscles in his back.

'Don't know about you, Boss, but every joint in my body aches. I don't think I slept a wink all night.'

'You've got to be joking. You've been snoring your bloody head off and, anyway, what time is it?'

'Just gone five o'clock.'

Before Dave had time to tackle the question of his snoring, Jenny knocked on the door once and immediately walked in, just as Dave had his hand down his trousers rearranging himself. Jenny glanced at the DI and just shook her head. 'They've found the van,' she announced triumphantly.

'About bloody time,' snapped the DCI. 'Sorry, Jenny, shouldn't take it out on you because the DI snores worse than a pig. The twats shouldn't have lost it in the first place. Where did they track it down?'

'Round the back of the Argos store down High Street,' said Jenny, bringing her hand up to her mouth to cover a yawn.

'Cheers, Jenny. Grab Tanya and tell her to get hold of Lee. I don't see why he shouldn't be deprived of sleep like the rest of us.'

'Ok. Sort out a car, will you, Dave? If you're not still over the limit, that is.' Marlowe smirked.

With the DI driving the Ford Mondeo pool car, complete with blues and twos, they pulled out of the Gordon Street nick. At that time of the morning, the traffic was almost non-existent. Only a handful of speeding taxis were on the road. They soon cleared a path as they saw the blue flashing lights in their rear view mirrors.

The speeding Mondeo left the Clive Sullivan Way at the Myton Street junction and passed through a red stop light. Gowan turned right opposite Silver Street, which would lead them to the High Street. Once on the High Street, they could see the intermittent flashing of blue lights in front of them.

DI Gowan pulled the Mondeo onto the waste ground, staying well clear of the immediate area around the abandoned van.

'Ok, let's do this properly. Tanya, check the boot and see if there are any SOCO suits.' The DI popped the boot and Tanya walked around the back of the vehicle. Much to her surprise, she found a full set of kit, enough for all of them.

Once they were all properly dressed in their protective suits, they moved across nearer to where the van had been cordoned off. The DCI pulled the hood over his head and was easing on the latex gloves as PC Raines came over.

'Sir,' he said, somewhat apprehensively, half expecting a bollocking for the debacle of the previous evening.

'Who found the van?' asked Marlowe as he scanned the area. The waste ground was the result of the demolition of an eighteenth century riverside warehouse. There had been more than a degree of controversy over the destruction of the listed build. The local historic society wanted the building restored to its former glory for use as a heritage centre. For the local council, the pound signs were a more attractive proposition. Consequently, the site was sold to a developer for a new hotel complex.

'We did, sir - me and my partner,' the PC replied, hoping the DCI wouldn't ask who lost it in the first place.

'And you are?'

'PC Raines. That's my partner stood next to the van.' Raines was feeling very uneasy.

'Right then, let's go and have a look.'

Marlowe, with the PC by his side, walked across and stopped short at the plastic tape.

'Has anyone touched the van?'

'No, sir. We thought it best not to, in the circumstances. We marked the immediate area off. No one's been past the tape.'

'Wise move' said Marlowe. By this time, the cavalry in the form of a van full of uniformed officers had arrived and begun a grid search of the waste ground.

'See if you can rustle up some hot drinks, son. We could all do with one,' Marlowe said to the pensive officer.

The DCI gave Dave Gowan a nod, held the tape up for him to go under and followed him through. Jenny and Tanya stayed outside the cordon and listened as the finding officers read from their notes. The uneven surface and the hard packed snow underfoot made the crossing to the van difficult.

One set of footprints led from the driving side of the van down to the river. They then turned around and walked away across the waste ground before disappearing at the pavement. Another set, belonging to PC Raines, circled the vehicle and retreated. Marlowe didn't want to contaminate the scene any further but, as usual, he couldn't wait for Karina and her team of SOCOs to arrive.

The hard overnight frost had transformed the van into a shimmering ice sculpture, reminiscent of those the DCI had seen on a visit to Toronto the previous winter. The pursuit vehicle had lost contact with the Transit just after eleven o'clock the previous evening; Marlowe glanced at his watch and did a quick calculation. Near enough six and a half hours had elapsed, he thought to himself.

The two officers walked towards the driver's side of the Transit. With his gloved hand, Marlowe rubbed away at the frost on the side window, clearing a patch the size of his fist. He peered into the cab.

'Hell, Dave, there's someone in there. You there!' He shouted to the nearest PC. 'Get this fucking door open, NOW!'

The DCI moved away from the vehicle and let the constable armed with a crowbar pass. Positioning the hooked end of the bar into the gap between the door and frame, he grunted as he levered the door open. It took him a full two minutes and a gallon of sweat to pop the door.

Once the door was free, Marlowe rushed forward and leant across the driver's seat to reach the man strapped in the passenger seat. The figure was stiff in his seat. His head lolled back and his skin was as pale as the frost that encircled him. His lips were light blue. The DCI put the fingers of his gloved hand on the neck of the stiff body and tried in vain to find a pulse. 'Shit,' he said to Dave Gowan. 'It looks like he's been dead all night.

Marlowe reached across the man carefully. Managing not to compromise the body, he released the lock on the passenger side door and unlocked it. With a latex gloved hand, DI Gowan heaved on the frosted door and pulled it open to its full extent. Even with the temperature still below freezing, the DI broke out into a cold sweat as he looked into the Transit. He could feel the colour draining from his face and perspiration trickling down his neck. He recognised the dead man. There was no doubt about it. He was one hundred percent certain. His appearance had changed, but it was definitely him.

'Phil,' the DI said, still looking into the van. Marlowe was surprised to hear the DI use his Christian name when they were on duty. Marlowe moved forward and stood beside the DI. 'What's the problem?' he asked puzzled.

'Did you get a good look at him?'

'No, not properly, why?'

'You didn't recognise him?'

'No, I've just said I didn't have a good look at him.'

'Take another look,' Dave Gowan could feel his legs shaking as he stepped backwards, giving the DCI space. Marlowe gave the DI a quizzical look as he stepped up to the open door. He rested a gloved hand on the door sill and leant inside the cab to give himself a clear view of the dead man.

'Oh, for fuck's sake, it's Karl.' Marlowe felt as drained as the DI looked. 'He looks about three stone lighter, but it's him,' Marlowe commented as he turned to face Gowan.

'What the hell has he got to do with this case? He's been on sick leave for the last eight months.' Gowan ran his hand across his mouth and face, feeling close to vomiting.

'The more immediate question is, why is he in the fucking van in the first place?' Marlowe speculated as he turned to face the DI. 'Dave, find out where the hell the SOCOs are. Tell Karina to stop pissing about and get her arse into gear, I want her here now. Jenny, I want this entire area sealed off completely. Get the road closed both ends, and nobody enters the site without my say so.'

Marlowe took his mobile phone from his pocket and pressed speed dial one, Superintendent Bulmer's mobile number. Without any apologies for the early morning call, Marlowe spoke into the receiver. 'Sir, it's Marlowe. We've got a situation... Yes, it is urgent, very fucking urgent!'

As the DCI put the mobile in his pocket, the SOCO team pulled onto the site.

'Over here,' Marlowe shouted to Karina.

Dave Gowan had somewhat recovered from the initial shock and could be heard speaking to Jenny. 'Tell Tanya to get the search team organised and tell Lee to get his skates on and find that PC with the coffee.'

* * *

Detective Sergeant Karl Gibson had just had it confirmed that he'd passed the East Riding Police Authority

Board. He was soon to become Detective Inspector Gibson. That same day tragedy struck the family. He'd been married to Jan for nineteen years. They had one child - a son. Life had been looking good for Gibson until six months ago, that is until their son found something else to depend on other than his parents – heroin. Then the shit really hit the fan.

* * *

Karina sorted her team out with assured authority as she climbed into her protective SOCO suit. 'Get the lights set, Peter. You're on the stills. Robin - video. Don't miss anything.'

'No sign of Brice joining us?' Gowan asked, having regained some of his composure.

'Sorry, you'll have to make do with me. Silly old goat's got his leg in pot from the ankle to his hip. Looks like a long job.' Karina pulled up the hood of her suit and tucked in her blonde hair. 'Right, I'm ready.'

Marlowe led Karina across the snowy waste to the still glistening Transit. The SOCO dropped down plastic footpads as they went. Both doors were still open. 'You opened these?' Karina demanded.

'Afraid so. Once we saw someone inside, there was no other option.' Marlowe moved to the side to allow Karina access.

'Would you wait at the other side of the tape, please, sir, until we've finished.'

The DCI backed away to let the dog see the rabbit. By the time they'd reached the vehicle, the well-practised SOCO team had assembled and turned on the portable spotlights, totally illuminating the scene. The generator whined away in the background.

Under the glare of the lights, the frost-covered van looked surreal. Karina's primary task was to examine the vehicle and its contents on site, including the body of DS Gibson. She reached down into the aluminium case she'd placed at her feet and took a torch from her pocket.

'Ok,' she said to herself. 'You can do this. Just try to avoid the eyes and get on with the job.' She took a deep breath, clicked on the torch and began her examination.

Marlowe walked back to where they had left the pool car. He pulled and heaved and worked his way out of his protective suit, throwing it into the boot when he was done. He was still having difficulty getting to grips with the situation.

From outside the cordon, he stood and watched the activity around the van. He pulled the collar of his coat tight around his neck and. With his hands deep in his pockets, he walked across the waste ground to the low wall at the river's edge and looked down into the mud. The tide was turning. As he looked up, he could see, on the opposite bank of the narrow river, Hull's state-of-the-art aquarium, The Deep, with it's the futuristic shape jutting out into the Humber like the bow of a ship. To his right, the massive structure of the River Hull flood barrier lit up the morning sky. The city had waited many years for a barrier to be erected to prevent the old town flooding.

The DCI took his hand out of his pocket along with his cigarettes and lighter. He shook out a Benson's, put it between his lips and lit it. The flame warmed his hands and

233

the nicotine calmed his mind. *So many questions*, he thought to himself as the young constable approached him with the elusive Styrofoam cup of coffee. Marlowe took a sip of the scalding liquid and grimaced at the bitter taste. One sip was enough and he tipped the remaining liquid over the wall into the river.

With his hands in his pockets again and the cigarette hanging from his lips, he turned around to face the activity. The beams from the search team's torches bounced off the snowy wasteland and artificially darkened the sky. It was so cold Marlowe was on the verge of shivering uncontrollably. When he exhaled, he could see his breath condensing in the air.

'What do you make of it?' Dave Gowan was by his side rubbing his hands together, trying to keep the circulation going.

'To be honest, I haven't got a fucking clue. Let's get back to the station and try to get our heads around this one. I think we've seen enough. There's no point hanging around here. We'll see what Karina comes up with.'

Marlowe led the way back to the pool car and climbed into the front passenger seat. Gowan walked around the back and slammed the boot lid closed. He kicked his feet on the door sill to clear off the snow and took the driving seat.

Chapter 24

Marlowe stood staring into the car park through the condensation running down his office window.

'What a mess,' he said to no one in particular as he turned around and dropped into the chair behind his desk. Dave and Jenny sat side-by-side on the office sofa. Tanya, Lee and Jonno squashed in where they could. Everyone was starting to thaw out and nursing a plastic cup of coffee from the vending machine.

'Any ideas what Karl could have been doing in the van?'

The DI spoke first, stretching his legs out in front of him, his arms clasped behind his head. 'To be honest, I haven't got a clue, but I'm starting to get a weird feeling about this.'

'You and me both,' Marlowe replied. He interlocked his fingers and stretched his arms out in front of him until the knuckle joints in his hands cracked. He laid his head back and yawned for England. It had been a long night and it was going to be an even longer day.

'Ok, questions: one, why was Karl in the van in the first place? Two, who was in the van with him? Three, is he connected to the other murders? Let's see if we can get some answers.' Marlowe studied the face of each officer in turn before settling on Tanya. 'Tanya, I want whatever Karina's got so far. Anything to get us started.'

As Marlowe finished speaking, Jenny felt her mobile vibrate in her pocket. 'Excuse me,' she said, retreating into the squad room to take the call. She came back into the office thirty seconds later. 'That was Karina. She's had a word with FME and they're giving priority to the post-mortem. It's scheduled for eleven this morning.'

'You go along with the DI to keep an eye on things. Report back to me as soon as it's over.' Needing a cigarette, Marlowe picked up a plastic pen and started chewing the end. With the pen still between his teeth, he turned. 'Tanya, I want you to get down to Karl's home. Take a couple of Uniforms with you. I want to know everything that's happened to him since he went sick.'

'Have you got an address?' she asked as she put down her coffee cup and stood up.

'Somewhere on Cottingham Road, near the University. Anyway, you won't need it. Jonno's going with you. He knows where to go.' Jonno nodded to the DCI and followed Tanya into the squad room.

'Sorry, son, you've drawn the short straw again,' Marlowe said to Lee. Check all the CCTV in the area. Where did the Transit come from? We know there were two men in the van when the dickheads lost it. Who was the other bloke?'

Marlowe's head was throbbing like a pneumatic drill. Once all the tasks were assigned, he went in search of drugs of a legal kind, Paracetamol.

* * *

'It's no good. He locked the door when he went out,' Tanya said. 'Get the enforcer from the car,' she told one of the Uniforms.

'Hang on a minute, there's no need for that,' protested Jonno, who then disappeared down the side of the house. Two minutes later, he was unlocking the front door from the inside.

'How did you manage that?'

'Janet, Karl's wife, was always losing her keys. They keep a spare set hidden around back in the shed. Probably haven't been used since she died.'

'Ok, lads, you take the upstairs,' Jonno instructed. 'We'll have a look around here.'

Once they were in the living room out of earshot of the officers upstairs, Tanya asked; 'What's the story with DS Gibson?'

'Yeah, of course. You never had the chance to meet him. You were still at Driffield when it all kicked off.' Tanya listened intently. Jonno kept searching as he told Tanya the tale. 'His son was a heroin user. Used to drive Karl and his wife barmy. They didn't know if they were coming or going.'

'How long was it going on?'

'Since he was fourteen, but the six months before the deaths it was horrendous for them.'

'Bit young to start on the hard stuff.'

'Yeah, well, wrong place, wrong time, and mixing with the wrong crowd. What can I say?' Jonno turned and stood in the doorway between the kitchen and the living room, leaning on the doorframe. 'They tried everything. Put him through rehab. It cost them a fortune, all for nothing. Even locked him in his room and tried to make him go cold turkey. When things got too bad, Karl went out and bought drugs for him, just to keep him off the streets.'

'Did it do any good?' asked Tanya as she rummaged through the kitchen drawers.

'For a short time, until he smashed the bedroom door down when they went out. When they came back, he'd sold half the contents of the house - the telly, video, DVD player, washing machine and even the three-piece suite. That was the final straw. They slung him out. They couldn't do it anymore.'

'Don't suppose anybody could blame them. It must have been rough.'

'Anyway, it was the day Karl's promotion to DI came through. He came home and found Janet tied to a chair in the kitchen with her head bashed in. The lad lay on the living room from an overdose. That's when he cracked up. All because of heroin.'

Tanya didn't say anything. She didn't know what to say. She walked into the hall and shouted up the stairs; 'Found anything yet?'

'No, not yet. Everything looks normal.'

'Hey, Tanya come and have a look at these.' Tanya about-turned into the living room where Jonno was holding a reporter's note pad and a grey document folder. He passed the folder over, still looking at the notepad.

'What ya got?'

'Not quite sure,' Jonno said, looking over the top of his reading glasses. 'It looks like a surveillance log - dealers' names, places and times, and there's a couple of names lined through. No prizes for guessing who.'

'You are kidding! I hope this doesn't mean what I think it does.'

'There's another two names heavily underlined.' His voice dropped almost to a whisper. 'Have a look who they are.' He passed it across.

'Bloody hell.'

Jonno nodded his agreement. 'Let's give the lads a chance to finish off upstairs first.'

Tanya took the papers out of the folder and started leafing through. 'As much as I don't want to believe it, I think we are on the right track, unfortunately.' The document she was holding was the lease agreement for a lock-up unit in the Hessle Road area.

'That's it, shout the lads down, we're going back now.'

* * *

Marlowe made time to get back to the Daisy for a quick shower, to change his shirt and to check up on Archie. Once again installed behind his desk, the DCI's face went deathly white when he was presented with evidence brought back by DC Lawson and DC Etherington. He brought his hands up to his face and rubbed it hard as if he was trying to bring the colour back to his pale complexion.

He slammed both fists down on the desk before him. 'Shit! I can't argue with evidence like this. Sorry to say, but it certainly doesn't look good. Tanya, go and find out what's keeping Lee with CCTV reports.'

Tanya took the hint, nodded, and went into the squad room, closing the door behind her as she went.

'I still can't believe it,' said Marlowe as he reached into the bottom drawer of his desk and brought out a half bottle of Johnny Walker Black Label and two glasses. He poured out two good measures and pushed one across the desk to Lawson. Jonno stood up from the small sofa, took half a dozen steps across the office and parked himself on the chair on the other side of Marlowe's desk.

'Cheers, Phil. I could do with this.' Jonno had also known Marlowe since they were constables together. Like DI Gowan, he never used the DCI's Christian name except in private.

'You tell Tanya the whole story?'

'Had no option. Best she heard it from me rather than listen to the gossip in the canteen.' Jonno picked up the whisky and sipped. The burning feeling it gave him was welcome, even though it was only ten-thirty in the morning.

'What do you reckon, Jonno, just between you and me and these four walls?'

'Vengeance, getting his own back on the shits that caused him to lose his family.' Jonno was thinking back to the funeral as he spoke. He remembered thinking how lost Karl had looked, sat on the front row of the crematorium with not one, but two coffins placed on trestles in front of him.

Marlowe picked up his drink and held it in both hands, swirling the liquid around the glass.

'That's my line of thinking. It's almost biblical. You could call it reprisal.'

'I still can't believe it. The more I think about it, well, it's just - I don't know.'

240

'It's bound to get out before too long, but let's try to keep a lid on it as long as we can.'

'Shouldn't be a problem. I've already had a word with the plods that came with us. Told them if they mentioned anything you'll have their balls for a necklace.'

'Another?' asked the DCI as he lifted the bottle and hovered it over Lawson's glass. Jonno didn't answer, just pushed his glass nearer the bottle.

The silence between the two didn't last long. TDC Kristianson knocked on the door of Marlowe's office and walked in. He was holding a batch of still photographs printed off from the CCTV cameras.

'Any luck?' Marlowe asked as Lee shuffled the photographs. The TDC reached across the desk and laid them out in time sequence.

'Eleven thirty four pm, the van was picked up near Cleveland Street and Holderness Road. There's no mistake - two people, one driving and someone in the passenger seat. Six minutes later, same van turning into Silver Street. You can see in this one that the patrol car goes straight past Silver Street.'

'The prats must have been half asleep to miss it. It could have made all the difference to Karl,' Marlowe mused.

'In this one, the Argos camera picked the van up precisely two minutes later as it turned onto the waste ground. There's no movement for eight minutes, then this bloke gets out and walks across to the river. On the VCR it looks as if he's throwing something into the mud.'

'The keys, probably,' said Jonno as he put down the glass.

'The best shot we have of him is this one walking across the waste ground to the road edge, and then he goes out of shot.'

Marlowe picked up his glasses and put them on. He reached across the desk to the glossy black and white eight by ten. 'Tell you what, he looks familiar.' He dropped it down and picked up another to study. 'Jonno, what do you think? Am I reading too much into this?' Marlowe passed it across. TDC Kristianson looked on, puzzled.

Jonno took the photograph from him. 'It could be, you know.'

'Thought maybe I was getting paranoid.'

'Who?' asked Lee.

'One of the Brothers Grimm - Pete Barnes. Go and tell the DI to come, will you?' Jonno followed Lee into the squad room.

DI Gowan had just walked in and was hanging his coat on the hanger.

'The Boss wants a word,' Jonno told him.

'Cheers, mate. I'll just grab a mug of tea.' Dave took a tea bag out of his drawer, dropped it into a semi-clean mug and made a quick visit to the vending machine to top it up with hot water.

'How's it going, Dave?' Cleeves enquired as he stood waiting to use the machine.

'Getting there, I don't like the way it's looking, but I can't do bugger all about that.' He squashed the tea bag about and added powdered milk. 'Just going in to see the PI. I'll keep you informed.'

'Take a seat, Dave. There's been some developments,' Marlowe began.

Careful not to slop his tea all over the place, Gowan set the mug down and sat opposite Marlowe. 'So I hear. I've been making enquiries myself. Remember Mr Ball?' the DCI looked a little puzzled until the DI clarified things. 'The bloke we pissed off when we bashed down his door?'

Marlowe cringed as he remembered. 'How can I forget? Go on.'

'Anyway, I thought it might be worth a visit. After creeping up to him and apologising for what seemed like forever, I showed him a photo of Karl.'

'And?' Marlowe asked with interest.

'No doubt about it, he was one hundred percent certain that it was Karl, who bought the van from him. He thought he had more hair and his face was fatter, but it was definitely Karl.'

Marlowe took off is spectacles and dropped them on the desk. 'You know, Dave, I'm getting more pissed off by the minute. Jonno and Tanya went round to Karl's and found a surveillance log, names of dealers, times and places and a lease agreement for a lockup. To top it all, Lee has CTTV pictures of someone who could be Pete Barnes walking away from the van with Karl in it. It can't get any worse, can it?' Gowan shrugged and yawned. They'd been on duty for almost twenty-four hours. 'I don't know about you, but I can't think straight. I know it's early and we haven't the post-mortem results yet, but let's call it a day here and now, and start afresh in the morning. Tell everyone, it's a seven o'clock start.'

'Right, then. I'll see you tomorrow. The lads will be pleased. It's doing all our heads in, this.' The DI went back to the squad room to pass on the message, tidied his desk and knocked off.

* * *

Marlowe knocked on the door. The warmth engulfed him as it opened.

'Come in, son,' Harry stood to one side to let Marlowe pass into the cosy front room. Archie galloped across and started fussing around Marlowe's feet. 'Sorry, lad, haven't had time to take Archie home. Joyce has had me painting the bathroom since first thing.'

'Don't go blaming me,' a voice shouted from the kitchen. 'Want a cuppa, Phil?'

'No thanks, Joyce, I've been out since the middle of the night and it's been a busy morning and all that. Just want to get cleaned up and get my head down. Got an early start again tomorrow.'

Joyce came through from the kitchen, wiping her soap sud hands, down her apron.

'Well, you know where we are if you want company.'

'It should be nice and warm on the Daisy. I went on board first thing when I picked up Archie and fed the boiler.' Harry struggled down to his knees and put on the dog's lead. He had an even harder struggle to get up again.

'Thanks, Joyce. I don't know what we'd do without you two.' Marlowe said his goodbyes and took a slow walk back to the boat, long enough for him to smoke one cigarette and to stand on the Beckside and have another while the dog took a leak.

'Bloody hell,' Marlowe said to the dog as he went into the Daisy's galley, 'it's like an oven in here.' Not that he was really complaining. It was welcoming to think at least someone still thought a bit about him, even if it was like stepping into a hothouse.

Archie soon settled down on his usual seat and Marlowe headed for a hot shower. He came back into the dinette feeling a little better after the recent events had been washed away. Dressed in his jogging trousers and top, Marlowe went through to the galley. He couldn't be bothered to cook and settled for a couple of slices of Scottish Cheddar cheese and biscuits. Keeping with the Scottish theme, he brought through from the galley with him a bottle of Bells whisky. He was in need of something a little stronger than wine this time and he had already started on the hard stuff in the office. Best not to mix things up. He was determined to sleep through the day and then through the night, with only a slight gap of consciousness in-between for Archie to get his constitutional.

He was baffled, puzzled and confused, not to say, at the very least, pissed off, and sleep was the only way for him to deal with this mood. The whisky went some way to soothing the tension, he couldn't grasp the full implications of his now deceased Detective Sergeant's activities. He dreaded what could come to light next. This afternoon the whisky was to offer a temporary solution and hopefully carry him through to the morning.

And what Archie wanted was another walk. He could see it in his face. His routine had been disturbed. Sorry, but he would have to wait. Marlowe had had enough of this day already.

Chapter 25

The heat in the main squad room was stifling. As ever, condensation ran down the windows. Marlowe wondered if the heating was on the blink and, on top of that, there was a strong smell of body odour.

The chat started to settle as he made his appearance. 'Right, cut out the noise and let's get started.'

The small CID room was full to capacity, overflowing with bodies borrowed from the uniform department, including Sergeant Cleeves who stood at the back intently listening. Not all the officers in the room were engaged in the investigation, but as the case did in some way effect more than a few officers, the DCI had made an exception to allow certain individuals to attend. The idea was basically to keep the station accurately informed of the events surrounding the death of a colleague rather than to allow unsavoury rumours to circulate.

The DCI stood with the white boards behind him. The latest distasteful crime scene photographs had already been added.

'As you and the rest of the station will know by now, the body of DS Gibson was found early yesterday morning.' The room took on a sombre note. The DCI stood and studied their faces. The Detective Sergeant had been at Gordon

Street for the past three years and, without doubt, was popular throughout the station.

'Jenny.' DS Bright stood and walked to the front to face the assembled officers. She nodded to the DCI who moved off-centre to give her room.

Jenny cleared her throat and took a deep breath.

'First off, the findings of the pathologist tell us death was due to hypothermia. Toxicology also revealed a large dose of Rohypnol in his system. It doesn't stop there. It also revealed a massive overdose of heroin, way over the top, enough to kill a cow.' Jenny could hear the murmurs going around the room. 'The heroin was administered orally. There were traces of the powder down the front of his jacket, on his lips and in his mouth. At this stage, how the Rohypnol got into his system is as yet to be determined.'

'How long had he been there, Sarge?' The question was from PC Raines

'It looks like he'd been in the van all night.' Raines looked sullen and glanced at his partner as DS Bright gave the answer. He felt responsible. If only they hadn't lost him, he thought to himself.

'Thank you, DS Bright.' Marlowe once more took centre-stage. 'At this point I would ask all of you not directly involved in the case to please leave.' The room remained quiet, barring the scraping of chairs and the odd whisper as the officers left. 'Lee, I wouldn't mind a coffee before we carry on.'

'Anyone else?' Kristianson asked.

The team chatted sporadically until Lee returned laden with a large tray of coffees.

The DCI picked up his mug and took a sip, almost spitting out the boiling drink as he scalded his lips. He gave Lee a murderous look.

'Sorry, Boss, temperature on the machine's all to cock.'

'It's not the only thing that's all to cock,' Marlowe mumbled under his breath. 'One thing is certain - the involvement of the Brothers Grimm, at the very least Pete.' Everyone in the room had come across the brothers at one time or another. 'The CCTV footage has been enhanced by Technical and it clearly shows him walking away from the vehicle.' Marlowe glanced sideways and noticed Karina standing by the glass door, Marlowe gave her the nod to come in. Karina perched on the edge of DI Gowan's desk and smoothed down her black skirt. The back of her hand brushed her blonde hair away from her eye. 'What have you got for me?' Marlowe demanded.

Karina spoke from where she was seated. 'First off, I can confirm that the tyre treads on the van are the same as those found at the scene of the second murder under the Wiltshire Road flyover. In the back cargo area, we found small pieces of polythene similar to that which the bodies were wrapped in.'

'What about the cab?' Marlowe asked impatiently.

'Plenty. Fingerprints galore. Also, someone had been doing a line or two of coke on the dashboard.'

Lee appeared to wake up. 'What about DNA?'

'We should have the results sooner rather than later.'

Dave Gowan turned to the SOCO. 'Come on Karina, stop pissing us about. Whose prints were they?'

249

She raised her eyebrows as she looked directly at him. 'I was coming to that.' Karina turned to face the DCI. 'At this stage we are presuming the van was owned by DS Gibson as we found his fingerprints all over the vehicle.' Karina could see that the DI was getting ever more agitated and speeded things up a little. 'Pete Barnes, his prints were everywhere in the cab too.'

'Positive?' asked Marlowe. 'No mistakes?'

'One hundred percent. Almost to the point of the ridiculous. He'd made no effort to try to wipe the cab clean.'

'The coke could explain that,' Tanya chipped in.

'Dave, get down to the Oakwood and pick Barnes up. Take Jonno and Lee with you.'

'Right, Boss. With a bit of luck he will still be in bed.' Gowan gave the others a nod, picked up his mug and drained the rest of his coffee.

The DCI continued. 'Jenny, you and Tanya are coming with me. We're going to have a look at the lockup. Ask Cleevsey if he's got a couple of plods free. Sort a pool car out, will you, Tanya? Come and get me when you're sorted.'

Marlowe left them to it and retreated to his office. He walked straight across to his desk, opened the top drawer and took out his cigarettes. 'Bollocks, it's too cold out there,' he said to himself as he looked at the ice in the car park. With the office window wide open, Marlowe lit the Benson's, letting the cold air in and blowing the blue smoke out. The past forty-eight hours had been eventful for sure. As he ran things over in his mind, he dreaded to think what they might find in the lock-up.

The DCI flicked the cigarette end away through the open window as Tanya stuck her head around the door. 'Car's sorted, Boss.'

'The lock-up's down Havelock Street, isn't it?' Marlowe searched through the folder on his desk and found the lease agreement they'd taken from the DS' house. He passed it across, walked around the desk and reached down his coat from the rack. 'Be with you in a minute.' Marlowe sighed as he reflected how quickly the evidence against his DS had mounted up. He slipped his arms into the sleeves and zipped up the front. The mobile in his pocket burst into the Nokia tune. 'Marlowe.'

The call was from the DI. 'No sign of him, Boss.'

'What about his brother?'

'Same. We're going to hang around a while, see who shows up.'

'Keep me posted.' He put his mobile away and headed for the car park with Tanya in tow.

'Good luck, Magnum, or perhaps not,' Cleeves said.

'Yeah, right, I'm with you there.' Marlowe punched in the code for the exterior door and they were gone.

* * *

'Take it easy, Tanya,' the DCI instructed as they turned onto Havelock Street. 'It should be somewhere on the left.'

Marlowe sat up front tapping his fingers on the dashboard, not realising he was doing it. He'd been at it since they'd left the station. If it had been anyone else, Jenny would have given him some verbal. A uniformed PC sat alongside her in the back, leaning forward, Marlowe

251

pulled the collar of his coat up as the constable breathed down his neck.

'There, sir. Think it's down this one.' The uniformed officer pointed a nicotine-stained finger over Marlowe's shoulder in the direction of an alleyway sandwiched between a boarded-over fish and chip shop and a fish smoke house. The alleyway was just wide enough for a large van.

Tanya eased the Peugeot into the alley and a patrol car with four officers on board followed directly behind her. The side brick wall bore the scars of the vehicles too wide to pass down. A sharp right turn at the bottom of the alley brought them into a large snow-covered concrete parking area. Six lock-up units with double timber doors faced them. Only one unit had tyre tracks leading to and from it.

Everyone gathered around the front of the pool car. Marlowe stood staring at the flaky green-painted wooden doors secured with a heavy-looking padlock.

'Go fetch the bolt cutters,' he told one of the uniformed officers. The constable walked around to the back of the car and opened the boot. He reached in and retrieved a large set of cutters. Marlowe nodded to the PC. 'Ok, son, go ahead.'

The constable stepped forward with the heavy tool and swung it up with both hands. The jaws fixed on the steel. He flexed the handles and squeezed the arms together. Snap. The lock fell to the floor.

Marlowe hesitantly stepped in front of the constable. He eased his gloved fingers into the gap between the doors and pulled. With the aid of a PC, he managed to pull the doors partly open against a growing mountain of snow. Jenny grabbed the door as well and, between the three of them, they yanked the door fully open.

Daylight flooded into the dingy interior. The rag over the grimy window flapped in the draft. The morning light reflected off the whitewashed walls. On the floor were two strategically placed squares of polythene. Standing on the sheeting were two identical wooden kitchen chairs, facing each other, placed six feet apart. One was vacant. Gary Barnes was taped to the other.

'Bloody hell, Tanya, ring for an ambulance.' Although Marlowe knew it was too late, he rushed forward and almost slipped flat on his face as his feet caught underneath the plastic sheeting. One of the PC's caught him by the elbow. With no time for thanks, they both made a move for Barnes. Marlowe shook his hands free of his gloves and put his fingers to Barnes' neck, feeling for a pulse. Unfortunately - or perhaps some might say 'fortunately' - Barnes was dead. 'No need for the ambulance to rush,' said Marlowe, shaking his head.

The body was fixed to the chair with what looked to be the same type of parcel tape as used in the other murders. The torso was attached tightly to the chair back and each of Barnes' legs was taped to a leg of the chair. Jenny crouched down directly in front of Barnes' corpse. His eyes were closed, with frozen tears clinging to his cheeks. The mouth was taped shut. Marlowe slowly moved around the back of the chair, being careful where he placed his feet on the plastic sheeting. He took a pen out of his pocket and gently brushed aside the spiked-up hair across the crown of Gary's head. There was no sign of a nail, not that it was any comfort to Barnes.

With her hands enclosed in a pair of latex gloves, Jenny examined the backs of Barnes' hands. 'Can't see any puncture marks on the back of the hands.'

'No nail either,' confirmed Marlowe as he put the pen back in his pocket. To say that everyone was stunned at the discovery was an understatement. Combined with the DS' recent activities, this was the icing on the cake. Everyone gave the body some space as they made as much of a search of the lock-up as they could without contaminating the evidence.

'Karina, it's Tanya. I'm with the Boss. I hope you're not planning anything special for the next few hours. We have another one...' She turned to Marlowe. 'SOCO will be here in ten minutes, Boss.'

'Cheers, Tanya. Right, you two, tape off the entire scene. I don't just mean the immediate area, the entire bloody street. And, Jenny, nobody in and especially nobody out until the door-to-doors have been carried out.'

Jenny took the Airwaves from her bag and spoke to Control. As she watched, the DCI left the lock-up with his cigarettes in his hand.

Tanya turned and looked at the DCI's worried face. 'What do you reckon's wrong with the PI?'

'Let's face it, if one of your DSs was literally going around knocking off dealers, I don't suppose you'd be happy either.' Jenny dropped the radio into her bag.

'Point taken,' Tanya said as she went to see what the Uniforms were up to.

Fifteen minutes later, Marlowe was still standing by the pool car, blowing blue smoke into the air as Karina and her team of crime scene technicians arrived.

* * *

The DCI and his team walked into the Gordon Street nick. Back behind his desk, he picked up the phone and dialled.

'Karina, as soon as you've got anything...,'

The chief SOCO cut him off mid-speech. 'You've only just left, sir. Give us a chance.' She hung up.

Marlowe knew he'd over-stepped the mark. He knew he'd be the first to be informed.

Tanya came into the office armed with yet more cups of coffee, this time accompanied by welcome bacon and sausage sarnies.

Jenny sat on Marlowe's small sofa with her sandwich in her hand.

'What do you reckon?' Tanya asked as she sat next to the DS, looking from one to the other.

'To be honest, I don't quite know what to make of it,' Marlowe replied.

Tanya had a theory of her own. 'You don't think he brought Gary there first with the intention of doing them both together?'

Marlowe pondered for a moment as he enjoyed the sarnie. 'You could have something there. I was thinking along similar lines. Somehow he manages to get Gary trussed up like a Bernard Mathews oven-ready and then goes looking for Pete.'

'Only things don't go quite to plan,' added Jenny.

'Pete susses out what's going on and turns the tables.'

'Next thing Karl has been over-dosed on "H", courtesy of Pete Barnes, who doesn't realise he's left his brother to die of hypothermia.' Tanya was feeling pleased with herself, her theory looked as if it had been accepted.

* * *

'How long are we going to sit here?' asked TDC Kristianson as he leaned forward between the front seats of the car.

'As long as it takes. Stop moaning,' the DI told him.

'I'm busting for a pee.'

'Bloody hell, Lee, just cross your legs, will you? Give it a rest or hang it out the door. Dave, over there.' Jonno nodded towards a figure coming away from the bookies.

'That's our boy. Let's give him a minute.'

Pete Barnes walked towards them as if he didn't have a care in the world, but he was an experienced enough villain to recognise an unmarked police car when he saw one. He casually did an about-turn and legged it.

'Shit, the bugger's seen us. Lee, with me!' Gowan called as he opened the passenger side door and dived for the pavement.

'Jonno, see if you can cut him off before he comes out the other side of the alley.'

Jonno threw the car into reverse and did a neat hand-brake turn. With wheels spinning, he headed off around the other side of the block.

Gowan panted and puffed as he gave chase. With Lee by his side, they pounded the potholed concrete path. The DI sidestepped the bollards at the entrance that were there to stop motorcyclists. Lee, the younger and fitter detective, soon took the lead, but Barnes was too far ahead. They didn't seem to be making any headway.

Pete came fast around the corner, glancing over his shoulder. He didn't realise the car parked at the entrance was an unmarked police vehicle and he kept going. When Jonno saw him coming, he simply opened the driver's side door and *bang!* Barnes went straight into the open door. Ten seconds later, the two detectives hove into view, stopped and applauded Jonno's quick thinking.

The DI walked slowly and deliberately over to the prone figure lying in an undignified position on the floor and crouched down beside him. 'You're... under arrest... ' said Gowan in between breaths as he gave the dazed Barnes a sly kick in the ribs. 'Nice and easy, Pete. Don't struggle.' He pulled his arms around his back and cuffed him none too gently.

* * *

Marlowe's spectacles steamed up as he and his team walked into the nick.

'Dave's got Barnes in the interview room, charging him as we speak,' Cleeves told him as he came through the custody suite door.

'Cheers, Trev,' Marlowe replied as he wiped his spectacles on his tie.

'I thought you would have been a bit more enthusiastic about it.'

'In normal circumstances I'd be over the moon, but it's not normal, is it? I've never known such a fucking mess.' He

257

walked away. Cleeves mumbled to himself, shrugged his shoulders and put his head back down into his paperwork.

Marlowe sat contemplating the morning's events. His respite didn't last very long when the phone rang. It was Superintendent Bulmer.

'Morning, sir... Yes, it appears we have reached a conclusion... I agree it doesn't show the force in a good light.' The DCI just wanted the conversation to end. He couldn't be bothered to listen to a lecture from Bulmer. 'Yes... not a very good result. Pete Barnes? He's in the interview room with DI Gowan... As soon as I know anything, I'll let you know.'

Marlowe stood by the open window with the inevitable cigarette, flicking his ash into the car park, when Dave Gowan knocked on the door and walked in grinning like a Cheshire cat. He dropped the charge sheet on the DCI's desk.

'No need to ask you how it went, then.' Marlowe tossed the butt into the air and closed the window.

'Hour and a half, shortest murder interview I've ever done. We told him how the evidence is stacked against him, the CCTV showing him at the scene, prints all over the van and the victim. We told him we are just waiting for confirmation on DNA. He just sat there saying nothing, then I dropped the bombshell.'

'Gary?' asked Marlowe.

He nodded in confirmation.

'That was it. He broke down and confessed to everything.'

'No loopholes. He did have a brief with him?' asked Marlowe.

'Oh yes, Spall, their usual brief. He kept advising Barnes to do the no comment thing. No matter what Spall said to him, Pete wouldn't listen. He took no notice and spurted it all out.'

'I suppose he felt it was his fault Gary died.'

'Suppose. You know, it's ironic: Karl told me he'd nail all the bastards responsible. I didn't think he meant it literally.'

Marlowe inwardly shivered as if someone had walked on his grave. On the surface, the outcome of the case was positive, but he felt no sense of jubilation at the inevitability of gaining a conviction on this one.

'Job well done, Dave. Let me have the paperwork as soon as you're sorted.'

* * *

Gowan still had plenty of paperwork to do. He had to cross the "T's" and dot the "I's", reports to complete and he had to clear the macabre images from the whiteboards. An hour later, Gowan once more knocked on the DCI's door.

'We're heading off to the George for a pint if you fancy it. First round's on me,' he said from the doorway.

'Bloody hell, Dave. I's not very often we hear that. How can I refuse? I'll see you in there.'

The DI went back into the CID room to round up the team for their celebratory drink. Marlowe could see the obligatory backslapping through his window. Socialising was the last thing he wanted to be doing considering the circumstances. He thought he'd give it a miss, then reconsidered. Perhaps he should make the effort. A quick pint with the team, leave some money behind the bar and make a discreet exit. Case closed.

* * *

Gowan and Bright were somewhat subdued after the initial jubilation. A colleague dying in those circumstances touched everyone. No matter how you tried to justify it, they had a colleague who had been responsible for three murders.

Marlowe thought he would throw in a morsel of light relief. He knocked on his office window and motioned for Gowan and Bright to come through. 'Dave, Jenny, give me a minute, will you?'

Gowan and Bright came into the office as requested.

'Take a seat. I won't keep you long.' Marlowe stood up from his chair, walked around the front of his desk and perched on the edge. The two officers looked on apprehensively, waiting for him to continue. 'As you're both aware, we've been short of a DS for longer than any of us would have liked and I appreciate the way in which you have coped without too much moaning.' Marlowe adjusted his position on the desk and continued. 'We have a new DS on the team as of today.'

'Anybody we know?' Gowan asked.

'All in good time.' Marlowe picked up the phone, spoke into the handset and stood with his arms folded across his chest.

Gowan and Bright turned when they heard a knock on the door and burst into raptures of laughter as DS Callum

McCraig came in, complete with the blow up doll under one arm. 'Dave, Jenny, meet your new colleagues.'

End.